Oliver Optic

The Yacht Club

The Young Boat-Builder

Oliver Optic

The Yacht Club
The Young Boat-Builder

ISBN/EAN: 9783337413101

Printed in Europe, USA, Canada, Australia, Japan

Cover: Foto ©berggeist007 / pixelio.de

More available books at **www.hansebooks.com**

THE YACHT CLUB SERIES.

THE YACHT CLUB;

OR,

THE YOUNG BOAT-BUILDER.

BY

OLIVER OPTIC,

AUTHOR OF "YOUNG AMERICA ABROAD," "THE ARMY AND NAVY SERIES,"
"THE WOODVILLE STORIES," "THE STARRY FLAG SERIES," "THE
BOAT CLUB STORIES," "THE LAKE SHORE SERIES,"
"THE UPWARD AND ONWARD SERIES,"
ETC., ETC.

WITH THIRTEEN ILLUSTRATIONS.

BOSTON:
LEE AND SHEPARD, PUBLISHERS.
NEW YORK:
LEE, SHEPARD AND DILLINGHAM.

TO

MY YOUNG FRIEND

CHARLES H. HASTINGS,

OF NEW YORK,

𝕿𝖍𝖎𝖘 𝕭𝖔𝖔𝖐 𝖎𝖘 𝕬𝖋𝖋𝖊𝖈𝖙𝖎𝖔𝖓𝖆𝖙𝖊𝖑𝖞 𝕯𝖊𝖉𝖎𝖈𝖆𝖙𝖊𝖉.

(8

PREFACE.

"The Yacht Club" is the second volume of the Yacht Club Series, to which it gives a name; and like its predecessor, is an independent story. The hero has not before appeared, though some of the characters of "Little Bobtail" take part in the incidents: but each volume may be read understandingly without any knowledge of the contents of the other. In this story, the interest centres in Don John, the Boat-builder, who is certainly a very enterprising young man, though his achievements have been more than paralleled in the domain of actual life.

Like the first volume of the series, the incidents of the story transpire on the waters of the beautiful Penobscot Bay, and on its shores. They include several yacht races, which must be more interesting to those who are engaged in the exciting sport of yachting, than to others. But the principal incidents are distinct from the aquatic narrative; and those who are not interested in boats and boating will find that Don John and Nellie Patterdale do not spend all their time on the water.

The hero is a young man of high aims and noble purposes: and the writer believes that it is unpardonable to awaken the interest and sympathy of his readers for any other than high-minded and well-meaning characters. But he is not faultless; he makes some grave mistakes, even while he has high aims. The most important lesson in morals to be derived from his experience is that it is unwise and dangerous for young people to conceal their actions from their parents and friends; and that men and women who seek concealment "choose darkness because their deeds are evil."

HARRISON SQUARE, BOSTON,
          May 22, 1873.

CONTENTS.

CHAPTER VII.

CHAPTER VIII.

CHAPTER IX.

CHAPTER X.

CHAPTER XI.

CHAPTER XII.

CHAPTER XIII.

CHAPTER XIV.

CHAPTER XV.

THE YACHT CLUB;

OR,

THE YOUNG BOAT-BUILDER.

CHAPTER I.

DON JOHN OF BELFAST, AND FRIENDS.

"WHY, Don John, how you frightened me!" exclaimed Miss Nellie Patterdale, as she sprang up from her reclining position in a lolling-chair.

It was an intensely warm day near the close of June, and the young lady had chosen the coolest and shadiest place she could find on the piazza of her father's elegant mansion in Belfast. She was as pretty as she was bright and vivacious, and was a general favorite among the pupils of the High School, which she attended. She was deeply absorbed in the reading of a story in one of the July magazines, which had

just come from the post-office, when she heard
a step near her. The sound startled her, it
was so near; and, looking up, she discovered
the young man whom she had spoken to close
beside her. He was not Don John of Austria,
but Donald John Ramsay of Belfast, who had
been addressed by his companions simply as
Don, a natural abbreviation of his first name,
until he of Austria happened to be mentioned
in the history recitation in school, when the
whole class looked at Don, and smiled; some of
the girls even giggled, and got a check for it;
but the republican young gentleman became a
titular Spanish hidalgo from that moment.
Though he was the son of a boat-builder, by
trade a ship carpenter, he was a good-looking,
and gentlemanly fellow, and was treated with
kindness and consideration by most of the sons
and daughters of the wealthy men of Belfast,
who attended the High School. It was hardly
a secret that Don John regarded Miss Nellie
with especial admiration, or that, while he was
polite to all the young ladies, he was particularly
so to her. It is a fact, too, that he blushed when
she turned her startled gaze upon him on the

piazza; and it is just as true that Miss Nellie colored deeply, though it may have been only the natural consequence of her surprise.

"I beg your pardon, Nellie; I did not mean to frighten you," replied Donald.

"I don't suppose you did, Don John; but you startled me just as much as though you had meant it," added she, with a pleasant smile, so forgiving that the young man had no fear of the consequences. "How terribly hot it is! I am almost melted."

"It is very warm," answered Donald, who, somehow or other, found it very difficult to carry on a conversation with Nellie; and his eyes seemed to him to be twice as serviceable as his tongue.

"It is dreadful warm."

And so they went on repeating the same thing over and over again, till there was no other known form of expression for warm weather.

"How in the world did you get to the side of my chair without my hearing you?" demanded Nellie, when it was evidently impossible to say anything more about the heat.

"I came up the front steps, and was walking around on the piazza to your father's library. I didn't see you till you spoke," replied Donald, reminded by this explanation that he had come to Captain Patterdale's house for a purpose. "Is Ned at home?"

"No; he has gone up to Searsport to stay over Sunday with uncle Henry."

"Has he? I'm sorry. Is your father at home?"

"He is in his library, and there is some one with him. Won't you sit down, Don John?"

"Thank you," added Donald, seating himself in a rustic chair. "It is very warm this after-noon."

Nellie actually laughed, for she was conscious of the difficulties of the situation—more so than her visitor. But we must do our hero—for such he is—the justice to say, that he did not refer to the exhausted topic with the intention of confining the conversation to it, but to introduce the business which had called him to the house.

"It is intensely hot, Don John," laughed Nellie.

"But I was going to ask you if you would not like to take a sail," said Donald, with a blush. "With your father," I mean, added he, with a deeper blush, as he realized that he had actually asked a girl to go out in a boat with him.

"I should be delighted to go, but I can't. Mother won't let me go on the water when the sun is out, it hurts my eyes so," answered Nellie; and the young man was sure she was very sorry she could not go.

"Perhaps we can go after sunset, then," suggested Donald. "I am sorry Ned is not at home; for his yacht is finished, and father says the paint is dry enough to use her. We are going to have a little trial trip in her over to Turtle Head, and, perhaps, round by Searsport."

"Is the Sea Foam really done?" asked Nellie, her eyes sparkling with delight.

"Yes, she is all ready, and father will deliver her to Ned on Monday, if everything works right about her. I thought some of your folks, especially Ned, would like to be in her on the first trip."

"I should, for one; but I suppose it is no use for me to think of it. My eyes are ever so much better, and I hope I shall be able to sail in the Sea Foam soon."

"I hope so, too. We expect she will beat the Skylark; father thinks she will."

"I don't care whether she does or not," laughed Nellie.

"Do you think I could see your father just a moment?" asked Donald. "I only want to know whether or not he will go with us."

"I think so; I will go and speak to him. Come in, Don John," replied Nellie, rising from her lolling-chair, and walking around the corner of the house to the front door.

Donald followed her. The elegant mansion was located on a corner lot, with a broad hall through the centre of it, on one side of which was the large drawing-room, and on the other the sitting and dining-rooms. At the end of the great hall was a door opening into the library, a large apartment, which occupied the whole of a one-story addition to the original structure. It had also an independent outside door, which opened upon the piazza; and opposite to it was a flight of steps, down to the gravel walk terminating at a gate on the cross street. People who came to see Captain Patterdale on business could enter at this gate, and go to the library without passing through the house. On the present occasion, a horse and wagon stood at the gate, which indicated to Miss Nellie that her father was engaged. This team had stood there for an hour, and Donald had watched it for half that time, waiting for the owner to leave, though he was not at all anxious to terminate the interview with his fair schoolmate.

Nellie knocked at the library door, and her father told her to come in. She passed in, while Donald waited the pleasure of the rich man in the hall.

He was invited to enter. Captain Patterdale was evidently bored by his visitor, and gave the young man a cordial greeting. Donald stated his business very briefly; but the captain did not say whether he would or would not go upon the trial trip of the Sea Foam. He asked a hundred questions about the new yacht, and it was plain that he did not care to resume the conversation with his visitor, who walked nervously about the room, apparently vexed at the interruption, and dissatisfied thus far with the result of his interview with the captain.

What would have appeared to be true to an observer was actually so. The visitor was one Jacob Hasbrook, from a neighboring town, and his reputation for honesty and fair dealings was not the

best in the world. Captain Patterdale held his
note, without security, for thirteen hundred and
fifty dollars. Hasbrook had property, but his
creditors were never sure of him till they were
paid. At the present interview he had astonished
Captain Patterdale by paying the note in full,
with interest, on the day it became due. But it
was soon clear enough to the rich man that the
payment was only a "blind" to induce him to
embark in a doubtful speculation with Hasbrook.
The nature and immense profits of the enterprise had been eloquently set forth by the
visitor, and his own capacity to manage it enlarged upon; but the nabob, who had made his
fortune by hard work, was utterly wanting in enthusiasm. He had received the money in payment of his note, which he had expected to lose,
or to obtain only after resorting to legal measures,
and he was fully determined to have nothing more
to do with the man. He had said all this as
mildly as he could; but Hasbrook was persist-
ent, and probably felt that in paying an honest
debt he had thrown away thirteen hundred and
fifty dollars.

He would not go, though Captain Patterdale

gave him sufficient excuse for doing so, or even for cutting his acquaintance. The rich man continued to talk with Don John, to the intense disgust of the speculator, who stood looking at a tin box, painted green, which lay on a chair. Perhaps he looked upon this box as the grave of his hopes; for it contained the money he had just paid to the captain—the wasted money, because the rich man would not embark with him in his brilliant enterprise, though he had taken so much pains, and parted with so much money, to prove that he was an honest man. He appeared to be interested in the box, and he looked at it all the time, with only an impatient glance occasionally at the nabob, who appeared to be trifling with his bright hopes. The tin chest was about nine inches each way, and contained the private papers and other valuables of the rich man, including, now, the thirteen hundred and fifty dollars just received.

Captain Patterdale was president of the Twenty-first National Bank of Belfast, which was located a short distance from his house. The tin box was kept in the vaults of the bank; but the owner had taken it home to examine some documents at his leisure, intending to return it to the bank before night.   As it was in the library when Mr. Hasbrook called, the money was deposited in it for safe keeping over night.

"I'm afraid I can't go with you, Donald," said Captain Patterdale, after he had asked him all the questions he could think of about the Sea Foam.

"I am sorry, sir; for Miss Nellie wanted to go, and I was going to ask father to wait till after sunset on her account," added the young man.

Mr. Hasbrook began to look hopeful; for the last remark of the nabob indicated a possible termination of the conversation.   Donald began his retreat toward the hall of the mansion, for he wanted to see the fair daughter again; but he had not reached the door before the captain called him back.

"I suppose your father wants some more money to-night," said he, feeling in his pocket for the key to open the tin box.

"He didn't say anything to me about it, sir," replied Donald; "I don't think he does."

Hasbrook looked hopeless again; for Captain Patterdale began to calculate how much he had paid, and how much more he was to pay, for the yacht.   While he was doing so, there was a

knock at the street door, and, upon being invited
to do so, Mr. Laud Cavendish entered the library
with a bill in his hand.

Mr. Laud Cavendish was a great man in his own
estimation, and a great swell in the estimation
of everybody else. He was a clerk or salesman
in a store; but he was dressed very elegantly for
a provincial city like Belfast, and for a "counter-
jumper" on six or eight dollars a week. He was
about eighteen years old, tall, and rather slender.
His upper lip was adorned with an incipient mustache, which had been tenderly coaxed and colored for two years, without producing any prodig-
ious result, though it was the pride and glory of
the owner. Mr. Cavendish was a dreamy young
gentleman, who believed that the Fates had made
a bad mistake in his case, inasmuch as he was
the son of an honest and industrious carpenter,
instead of the son and heir of one of the nabobs
of Belfast. He believed that he was fitted to
adorn the highest circle in society, to shine
among the aristocracy of the city, and it was a
cruel shame that he should be compelled to work
in a store, weigh out tea and sugar, carry goods
to the elegant mansions where he ought to be ad-

mitted at the front, instead of the back, door, collect bills, and perform whatever other service might be required of him. The Fates had blundered and conspired against him; but he was not without hope that the daughter of some rich man, who might fall in love with him and his mustache, would redeem him from his slavery to an occupation he hated, and lift him up to the sphere where he belonged. Laud was "soaring after the infinite," and so he rather neglected the mundane and practical, and his employer did not consider him a very desirable clerk.

Mr. Laud Cavendish came with a bill in his hand, the footing of which was the sum due his employer for certain necessary articles just delivered at the kitchen door of the elegant mansion. Captain Patterdale opened the tin box, and took therefrom some twenty dollars to pay the bill, which Laud receipted. Mr. Hasbrook hoped he would go, and that Don John would go; and perhaps they would have gone if a rather exciting event had not occurred to detain them.

"Father! father!" exclaimed Miss Nellie, rushing into the library.

"What's the matter, Nellie?" demanded her

father, calmly; for he had long been a sea captain, and was used to emergencies.

"Michael has just dropped down in a fit!" gasped Nellie.

"Where is he?"

"In the yard."

Captain Patterdale, followed by his three visitors, rushed through the hall, out at the front door, near which the unfortunate man had fallen, and, with the assistance of his companions, lifted him from the ground. Michael was the hired man who took care of the horses, and kept the grounds around the elegant mansion in order. He was raking the gravel walk near the piazza where Nellie was laboring to keep cool. As we have hinted before, and as Nellie and Don John had several times repeated, the day was intensely hot. The sun where the man worked was absolutely scorching, and the hired man had experienced a sun-stroke. Captain Patterdale and his visitors bore him to his room in the L, and Don John ran for the doctor, who appeared in less than ten minutes. The visitors all did what they could, Mr. Laud Cavendish behaving very well. Michael's wife and other friends soon arrived, and there was nothing more for Laud to do. He went down stairs, and, finding Nellie in the hall, he tried to comfort her; for she was very much concerned for poor Michael.

"Do you think he will die, Mr. Cavendish?" asked she, almost as much moved as though the poor man had been her father.

"O, no! I think he will recover. These Irishmen have thick heads, and they don't die so easily of sun-stroke; for that's what the doctor says it is," replied Laud, knowingly.

Nellie thought, if this was a true view of *coup de soleil*, Laud would never die of it. She thought this; but she was not so impolite as to say it. She asked him no more questions; for she saw Don John approaching through the dining-room.

"Good afternoon, Miss Patterdale," said Laud, with a bow and a flourish, as he retired towards the library, where he had left his hat.

In a few moments more, the rattle of the wagon, with which he delivered goods to the customers, was heard as he drove off. Don John came into the hall, and Nellie asked him ever so many questions about the condition of Michael, and what the doctor said about him; all of which the young man answered to the best of his ability.

"Do you think he will die, Don John?" she asked.

"I am sure I can't tell," replied Donald; "I hope not."

"Michael is real good, and I am so sorry for him!" added Nellie.

But Michael is hardly a personage in our story, and we do not purpose to enter into the diagnosis of his case. He has our sympathies on the merit of his sufferings alone, and quite as much for Nellie's sake; for it was tender, and gentle, and kind in her to feel so much for a poor Irish laborer. While she and Donald were talking about the case, Mr. Hasbrook came down stairs, and passed through the hall into the library, where he, also, had left his hat. In a few moments more the rattle of his wagon was heard, as he drove off, indignant and disgusted at the indifference of the nabob in refusing to take an interest in his brilliant enterprise. He was angry with himself for having paid his note before he had enlisted the payee in his cause.

"How is he, father?" asked Nellie, as Captain Patterdale entered the hall.

"The doctor thinks he sees some favorable symptoms."

"Will he die?"

"The doctor thinks he will get over it. But he wants some ice, and I must get it for him."

"I suppose you will not go in the Sea Foam now?" asked Donald.

"No; it is impossible," replied the captain, as he passed into the dining-room to the refrigerator.

The father was like the daughter; and though he was a *millionnaire*, or a *demi-millionnaire*—we don't know which, for we were never allowed to look over his taxable valuation—though he was a nabob, he took right hold, and worked with his own hands for the comfort and the recovery of the sufferer. It was creditable to his heart that he did so, and we never grudge such a man his "pile," especially when he has earned it by his own labor, or made it in honorable, legitimate business. The captain went up stairs again with a large dish of ice, to assist the doctor in the treatment of his patient.

Donald staid in the hall, talking with Miss Nellie, as long as he thought it proper to do so, though not as long as he desired, and then entered the library where he, also, had left his hat. Perhaps it was a singular coincidence that all three of the visitors had left their hats in that room; but then it was not proper for them to sit with their hats on in the presence of such a magnate as Captain Patterdale, and no decent man would stop for a hat when a person had fallen in a fit.

Captain Patterdale's hat was still there; and, unluckily, there was something else belonging to him which was not there.

CHAPTER II.

ABOUT THE TIN BOX.

CAPTAIN PATTERDALE worked with the doctor for a full hour upon poor Michael, who at the end of that time opened his eyes, and soon declared that he was "betther entirely." He insisted upon getting up, for it was not "the likes of himself that was to lay there and have his honor workin' over him." But the doctor and the nabob pacified him, and left him, much improved, in the care of his wife.

"How is he, Dr. Wadman?" asked the sympathizing Nellie, as they came down stairs together.

"He is decidedly better," replied the physician.

"Will he die?"

"O, no; I think not. His case looks very hopeful now."

"I thought folks always died with sunstroke," said Nellie, more cheerfully.

"No; not unless their heads are very soft," laughed the doctor.

"Well, I shouldn't think Laud Cavendish would dare to go out when the sun shines," added the fair girl, with a snap of her bright eyes.

"It isn't quite safe for him to do so. Unfortunately, such people don't know their own heads. I will come in again after tea," said the doctor, as he went out of the house, at the front door; for he had not left his hat in the library.

"I am so glad Michael is better!" continued Nellie. "When I saw him drop, I felt as cold as ice, and I was afraid I should drop too before I could get to the library."

"Did you see him fall, Nellie?" asked her father.

"Yes; he gave a kind of groan, and then fell; he was—"

"Gracious!" exclaimed Captain Patterdale, interrupting her all of a sudden.

He turned on his heel, and walked rapidly into the library. Nellie was startled, and was troubled with a suspicion that her father had a *coup de soleil,* or *coup de* something-else; for he did not often do anything by fits and starts. She followed him into the library. It was a fact that the captain had left his hat there; but it was not for this article, so necessary in a hot day, that he hastened thus abruptly into the room. Nellie found him flying around the apartment in a high state of excitement for him. He was looking anxiously about, and seemed to be very much disturbed.

"What in the world is the matter, father?" asked Nellie.

"Where is your mother?"

"She has gone over to Mrs. Rodman's."

"Hasn't she been back?"

"No, certainly not; I was just going over to tell her what had happened to Michael, when you came down."

"Who has been in here, Nellie?"

"I don't know that anybody has. I haven't seen any one. What's the matter, father? what in the world has happened?"

"I left my tin box here when I went out to see to Michael, and now it is gone," answered Captain Patterdale, anxiously. "I didn't know but that your mother had come in and taken care of it.”

“The tin box gone?” exclaimed Nellie. “Why, what can have become of it?”

“That is just what I should like to know,” added the captain, as he renewed his search in the room for the treasure chest.

It was not in the library, and then he looked in the great hall and in the little hall, in the drawing-room, the sitting-room, and the dining-room; but it was not in any of these. He knew he had left it on the chair near where he was sitting when he went out of the room. Then he examined the spring-lock on the door of the library which led into the side street. It was closed and securely fastened. The door shut itself with a patent invention, and when shut it locked itself, so that anybody could get out, but no one could get in unless admitted.

“Where were you when I was up stairs, Nellie?” asked Captain Patterdale, as he seated himself in his arm-chair, to take a cool view of the whole subject.

“I was in the hall most of the time,” she replied.

"Who has been in the library?"

"Let me see; Laud Cavendish came down first, and went out through the library."

The captain rubbed his bald head, and seemed to be asking himself whether it was possible for Mr. Laud Cavendish to do so wicked a deed as stealing that tin box. He did not believe the young swell had the baseness or the daring to commit so great a crime. It might be, but he could not think so.

"Who else has been in here?" he inquired, when he had hastily considered all he knew about the moral character of Laud.

"That other man who was with you—I don't know his name—the one that was here when I came in with Don John."

"Mr. Hasbrook."

"He went out through the library. I thought he looked real ugly too," added Nellie. "He kept fidgeting about all the time I was here."

"And all the time he was here himself. He went out through the library—did he?"

"Yes, sir."

Captain Patterdale mentally overhauled the character of Mr. Hasbrook. It was unfortunate

for his late debtor that his character was not first
class, and between him and Laud Cavendish the
probabilities were altogether against Hasbrook.
He had evidently been vexed and angry because
he failed to carry his point, and his cupidity
might have been stimulated by revenge. But the
captain was a fair and just man, and in a matter of
this kind, involving the reputation of any person,
he kept his suspicions to himself.

"Who else has been in the library, Nellie?"
he asked.

"No one but Don John," replied she. And
whatever Laud or Hasbrook might have done in
wickedness, Nellie had too much regard for her
friend and schoolmate to admit for one instant the
possibility of his doing anything wrong, much less
his committing so gross a crime as the stealing
of the tin box and its valuable contents.

Captain Patterdale was hardly less confident of
the integrity of Donald. Certainly it was not
necessary to suspect him when the possibilities of
guilt included two such persons as Laud and Hasbrook. Donald was rather distinguished, in school
and out, as a good boy, and he ought to have the
full benefit of his reputation.

3

"You don't think Don John took the box—do you, father?" asked Nellie, as her father was meditating on the circumstances.

"Certainly not, Nellie," protested the captain, warmly; "I don't know that anybody has taken it."

"I know Don John would not do such a thing."

"I don't believe he would."

"I know he would not."

Her father thought she was just a little more earnest in her uncalled-for defence of the young man than was necessary, and for the first time in his life it occurred to him that she was more interested in him than he wished her to be; for, as Donald was only the son of a poor boat-builder, such a strong friendship might be embarrassing in the future. However, this was only the shadow of a passing thought, which divided his attention only for a moment. The loss of the tin box was the question of the hour, and "society" topics were not just then in order.

"I have no idea that Don John took the box," replied Captain Patterdale. "I am more willing to believe either of the other two who were in the library took it than that he did. But he was the last of the three who went out through this room. He may be able to give me some information, and I will go down and see him. He and his father were going off in the new yacht—were they not?"

"Yes, sir."

"You need not say a word about the box to any one, Nellie, nor even that it is lost," added the captain. "If I do not find it, I shall employ a skilful detective to look it up, and he may prefer to work in the dark."

"I will not mention it, father," replied Nellie. "What was in the box? Was it money?"

"I put thirteen hundred and fifty dollars into it, but I took out twenty to pay the bill that Laud brought. It contains my deeds, leases, policies of insurance, and my notes, and these papers are really more valuable to me than the money. Luckily, my bonds and securities are in another box, in the vault of the bank."

"Then you will lose over thirteen hundred dollars if you don't find the box?"

"More than that, I am afraid, for I shall hardly be able to collect all the money due on the notes if I lose them," replied the captain, as he left the house.

He walked down to the boat shop of Mr. Ramsay. It was on the shore, and near it was the house in which the boat-builder lived. Neither Don John nor his father was at the shop, but a sloop yacht, half a mile out in the bay, seemed to be the Sea Foam. She was headed towards the shore, however, and Captain Patterdale seated himself in the shade of the shop to await its arrival, though he hardly expected to obtain any information in regard to the box from Donald. While he was sitting there, Mr. Laud Cavendish appeared with a large basket in his hand. The counter-jumper started when he turned the corner of the shop, and saw the nabob seated there.

"Going a-fishing?" asked the captain.

"Yes, sir; I 'm going over to Turtle Head to camp out over Sunday," replied Laud. "How is Michael, sir?"

"He is much better, and is doing very well."

"I'm glad of it," added Laud, as he carried his basket down to a sail-boat which was partly aground, and deposited it in the forward cuddy.

Captain Patterdale wanted to talk with Laud, but he did not like to excite any suspicions on his part. If the young man had taken the box he would not be likely to go off on an island to stay over Sunday. Besides, it was evident from the position of the boat, and the fact that it contained several articles necessary for a fishing excursion, in addition to those in the basket, that Laud had made his arrangements for the trip before he visited the library of the elegant mansion. If he had taken the box, he would probably have changed his plans. It was not likely, therefore, that Laud was the guilty party.

"Are you going alone?" asked the captain, walking down the beach to the boat.

"Yes, sir; I couldn't get any one to go with me. I tried Don John, but he won't go off to stay over Sunday," replied Laud, with a sickly grin.

"I commend his example to you. I don't think it is a good way to spend Sunday."

"It's the only time I can get to go. I've been trying to get off for a month."

"Saturday must be a bad time for you to leave," suggested the captain.

"It is rather bad," added Laud, as he shoved off the bow of the boat, for he seemed to be in haste to get away.

"By the way, Laud, did you notice a tin box

in my library when you were there this afternoon?" asked the nabob, with as much indifference in his manner and tone as he could command.

"A tin box?" repeated Laud, busying himself
with the jib of the sail-boat.

"Yes; it was painted green."

"I don't remember any box," answered Laud.

"Didn't you see it? I opened it to take out
the money I paid you."

"I didn't mind. I was receipting the bill
while you were getting the money ready. You
know I sat down at your desk."

"Yes; I know you did; but didn't you see the
box?"

"No, sir; I don't remember seeing any box,"
said Laud, still fussing over the sail, which certainly did not need any attention.

"You went out through the library when you
came down from Michael's room—didn't you?"
continued the captain.

"Yes, sir; I did. I left my hat in there."

"Did you see the box then?"

"Of course I didn't. If I had, I should have
remembered it," replied Laud, with a grin. "I
just grabbed my hat, and ran, for I had been

in the house some time; and I got a blessing for being away so long when I went back to the store.''

''You didn't see the box, then?''

''If it was there, I suppose I saw it; but I didn't take any notice of it. Why? is the box lost?''

''I want to get another like it. Haven't you anything of the sort in the store?''

''We have some cake and spice boxes. They are tin, and painted on the outside.''

''Those will not answer the purpose. It's a very hot day,'' added the captain, as he wiped the perspiration from his face, and walked back to the shade of the shop.

Mr. Laud Cavendish stepped into the sail-boat, hoisted the sails, and shoved her off into deep water with an oar. Captain Patterdale thought, and then he did not know what to think. Was it possible Laud had not noticed that tin box, which had, been on a chair out in the middle of the room? If he had not, why, then he had not; but if he had Laud had more cunning, more self-control, and more ingenuity than the captain had ever given him the credit, or the discredit, of possessing, for there was certainly no sign of guilt in his tone or his manner, except that he did not look the inquirer square in the face when he answered his questions, though some guilty people can even do this without wincing.

Captain Patterdale watched the departing and the approaching boats, still considering the pos-sible relation of Laud Cavendish to the tin box. If the fellow had stolen it, he would not go off on an island to stay over Sunday, leaving the box behind to betray him; and this argument seemed to be conclusive in his favor. The captain had looked into the boat, and satisfied himself that the box was not there; unless it was in the bas-ket, which appeared to contain so many other things that there was no room for it. On the whole, the captain was willing to acquit Mr. Laud Cavendish of the act, partly, perhaps, be-cause this had been his first view of the matter. It was more probable that Hasbrook, angry and disappointed at his failure, had put the box into his wagon, and returned to the neighboring town, where, as before stated, his reputation was not first class, though, perhaps, not many people be-lieved him capable of stealing outright, without the formality of getting up a mining company, or making a trade of some sort. But Donald had been the last of the trio of visitors who passed through the library, and the captain wanted to see him.

The Sea Foam, with snowy sails just from the loft, and glittering in her freshly-laid coat of white paint, ran up to a wharf just below the boat shop. Donald was at the helm, and he threw her up into the wind just before she came to the pier, so that when she forged ahead, with her sails shaking in the wind, her head came up within a few inches of the landing-place. Mr. Ramsay fended her off, and went ashore with a line in his hand, which he made fast to a ring. Captain Patterdale walked around to the wharf, as soon as he saw where she was to make a landing.

"Well, how do you like her, Sam?" said Donald to a young man of his own age in the standing-room with him.

"First rate; and I hope your father will go to work on mine at once," replied the passenger.

"You will lay down the keel on Monday — won't you, father?"

"What?" asked Mr. Ramsay, who had seated himself on a log on the wharf.

"You will lay down the keel of the boat for Mr. Rodman on Monday—won't you?" repeated Donald.

"Yes, if I am able; I don't feel very well to-day." And the boat-builder doubled himself up, as though he was in great pain.

The young man in the standing-room of the Sea Foam was Samuel Rodman, a schoolmate of Donald, whose father was a wealthy man, and had ordered another boat like the Skylark, which had been the model for the new yacht. He had come down to see the craft, and had been invited to take a sail in her; but an engagement had prevented him from going as far as Turtle Head, and the boat-builder and his son had returned to land him, intending still to make the trip. By this time Captain Patterdale had reached the end of the wharf. He went on board of the Sea Foam, and looked her over with a critical eye, and was entirely satisfied with her. He was invited to sail in her for as short a time as he chose, but he declined.

"By the way, Donald, did you see the green tin box when you were in my library this afternoon?" he asked, when all the topics relating to the yacht had been disposed of.

"Yes, sir; I saw you take some money from it," replied Donald.

"Then you remember the box?"

"Yes, sir."

"Did you notice it when you came out—I mean, when you left the house?"

"I don't remember seeing it when I came out," answered Donald, wondering what these questions meant.

"I want to get another box just like that one. Did you take particular notice of it?"

"No, sir; I can't say I did."

"You didn't stay any time in the library after you came down from Michael's room, did you?"

"No, sir; I only went for my hat, and didn't stay there a minute."

"And you didn't notice the tin box?"

"No, sir; I didn't see it at all when I came out."

"Then of course you didn't see any marks upon it," added the captain, with a smile.

"If I didn't see the box, I shouldn't have been likely to see the marks," laughed Donald. "What marks were they, sir?"

"It's of no consequence, if you didn't see them,

The box was in the library—wasn't it?—when you went out."

"I don't know whether it was or not. I only know that I don't remember noticing it," said Donald, who thought the captain's question was a very queer one, after those he had just answered.

The nabob was no better satisfied with Donald's answers than he had been with those of Laud Cavendish, except that the former looked him full in the face when he spoke. He obtained no information, and went home to seek it at other sources.

"I think I won't go out again, Donald," said Mr. Ramsay, when Captain Patterdale had left. "I don't feel very well, and you may go alone."

"Do you feel very sick, father?" asked the son, in tones of sympathy.

"No; but I think I will go into the house and take some medicine. You can run over to Turtle Head alone," added the boat-builder, as he walked towards the house.

"Can't you go any how, Sam?" said Donald, turning to his friend.

"No, I must go home now. I have to drive over

to Searsport after my sister,'' replied Sam, as he left the yacht, and walked up the wharf.

Donald hoisted the jib of the Sea Foam, shoved off her head, and laid her course, with the wind over the quarter, for Turtle Head—distant about seven miles.

CHAPTER III.

THE YACHT CLUB AT TURTLE HEAD.

THE Sea Foam was a sloop yacht, thirty feet in length, and as handsome as a picture in an illustrated paper, than which nothing could be finer. It was a fact that she had cost twelve hundred dollars; but even this sum was cheaper than she could have been built and fitted up in Boston or Bristol. She was provided with everything required by a first class yacht of her size, both for the comfort and safety of the voyager, as well as for fast sailing. Though Mr. Ramsay, her builder, was a ship carpenter, he was a very intelligent and well-read man. He had made yachts a specialty, and devoted a great deal of study to the subject. He had examined the fastest craft in New York and Newport, and had their lines in his head. And he was a very ingenious man, so that he had the tact to make the most of small spaces, and to economize every spare inch in lockers, closets, and stow-holes for the numerous articles required in a pleasure craft. He had learned his trade as a ship carpenter and joiner in Scotland, where the mechanic's education is much more thorough than in our own country, and he was an excellent workman.

The cabin of the Sea Foam was about twelve feet long, with transoms on each side, which were used both as berths and sofas. They were supplied with cushions covered with Brussels carpet, with a pillow of the same material at each end. Through the middle, fore and aft, was the centre-board casing, on each side of which was a table on hinges, so that it could be dropped down when not in use. The only possible objection to this cabin, in the mind of a shoreman, would have been its lack of height. It was necessarily "low studded," being only five feet from floor to ceiling, which was rather trying to the perpendicularity of a six-footer. But it was a very comfortable cabin for all that, though tall men were compelled to be humble within its low limits.

It was entered from the standing-room by a single step covered with plate brass, in which the

name of the yacht was wrought with bright copper
nails.   On each side of the companion-way was a
closet, one of which was for dishes, and the other
for miscellaneous stores.   The trunk, which readers away from boatable waters may need to be
informed is an elevation about a foot above the
main deck, to afford head-room in the middle of
the cabin, had three deck lights, or ports, on
each side.   At one end of the casing of the centre-
board was a place for the water-jar, and a rack
for tumblers.   In the middle were hooks in the
trunk-beams for the caster and the lantern.   The
brass-covered step at the entrance was movable,
and when it was drawn out it left an opening into
the run under the standing-room, where a considerable space was available for use.   In the centre
of it was the ice-chest, a box two feet square,
lined with zinc, which was rigged on little
grooved wheels running on iron rods, like a
railroad car, so that the chest could be drawn
forward where the contents could be reached.
On each side of this box was a water-tank, holding thirty gallons, which could be filled from the
standing-room.   The water was drawn by a faucet
lower than the bottom of the tank in a recess at

one side of the companion-way. The tanks were connected by a pipe, so that the water was drawn from both. At the side of the step was a gauge to indicate the supply of fresh water on board.

Forward of the cabin, in the bow of the yacht, was the cook-room, with a scuttle opening into it from the forecastle. The stove, a miniature affair, with an oven large enough to roast an eight-pound rib of beef, and two holes on the top, was in the fore peak. It was placed in a shallow pan filled with sand, and the wood-work was covered with sheet tin, to guard against fire. Behind the stove was a fuel-bin. On each side of the cook room was a shelf eighteen inches wide at the bulk-head and tapering forward to nothing. Under it were several lockers for the galley utensils and small stores. The room was only four feet high, and a tall cook in the Sea Foam would have found it necessary to discount himself. On the foremast was a seat on a hinge, which could be dropped down, on which the "doctor" could sit and do his work, roasting himself at the same time he roasted his beef or fried his fish. Everything in the cook-room and the cabin, as well as on deck, was neat and nice. The cabin was cov-

ered with a handsome oil-cloth carpet, and the
wood was white with zinc paint, varnished, with
gilt moulding to ornament it. Edward Patterdale, who was to be the nominal owner and the
real skipper of this beautiful craft, intended to
have several framed pictures on the spaces between the deck lights, a clock in the forward end
over the cook-room door, and brass brackets for
the spy-glass in the companion-way.

On deck the Sea Foam was as well appointed
as she was below. Her bowsprit had a gentle
downward curve, her mast was a beautiful spar,
and her topmast was elegantly tapered and set
up in good shape. Unlike most of the regular
highflyer yachts, her jib and main-sail were
not unreasonably large. Mr. Ramsay did not intend that it should be necessary to reef when it
blew a twelve-knot breeze, and, like the Skylark,
she was expected to carry all sail in anything
short of a full gale. But she was provided with
an abundance of "kites," including an immense
gaff-topsail, which extended on poles far above
the topmast head, and far beyond the peak, a
balloon-jib, a jib-topsail, and a three-cornered
studding-sail. The balloon-jib, or the jib-topsail,

was bent on with snap-hooks when it was needed, for only one was used at the same time. These extra sails were to be required only in races, and they were kept on shore. One stout hand could manage her very well, though two made it easier work, and six were allowed in a race.

Donald seated himself in the standing-room, with the tiller in his right hand. As soon as he had run out a little way, his attention was excited by discovering three other sloop yachts coming down the bay. In one of them he recognized the Skylark, and in another the Christabel, while the third was a stranger to him, though he had heard of the arrival that day of a new yacht from Newport, and concluded this was she. He let off his sheet, and ran up to meet the little fleet.

"Sloop, ahoy!" shouted Robert Montague, from the Skylark, as Donald came within hailing distance.

"On board the Skylark!" replied the skipper of the Sea Foam.

"Is that you, Don John?"

"Ay, ay."

"What sloop is that?" demanded Robert.

"The Sea Foam."

"Where bound?"

"Over to Turtle Head."

"We are bound there; come with us."

"Ay ay."

"Hold on a minute, Don John," shouted some one from the Christabel.

Each of the yachts had a tender towing astern, and that from the Christabel, with five boys in it, immediately put off, and pulled to the Sea Foam.

"Will you take us on board, Don John?" asked Gus Barker, as the tender came alongside.

"Certainly; I'm glad to have your company," replied Donald, who had thrown the yacht up into the wind.

Three of the party in the tender jumped upon the deck of the Sea Foam, and the boat returned to the Christabel. Each of the yachts appeared to have half a dozen or more on board of her, so that there was quite a party on the way to Turtle Head. The sloops filled away again, the Skylark and the new arrival having taken the lead, while the other two were delayed.

"What sloop is that with the Skylark?" asked Donald.

"That's the Phantom. She got here from Newport this forenoon. Joe Guilford's father bought her for him. She is the twin sister of the Skylark, and they seem to make an even thing of it in sailing," replied Gus Barker.

"You have quite a fleet now," added Donald.

"Yes; and we are going to form a Yacht Club. We intend to have a meeting over at Turtle Head. Will you join, Don John?"

"I haven't any boat."

"Nor I, either. All the members can't be skippers," laughed Gus. "I am to be mate of the Sea Foam, and that's the reason I wanted to come on board of her."

"And I am to be one of her crew," added Dick Adams.

"And I the steward," laughed Ben Johnson. "I am going down into the cook-room to see how things look there."

"You will join—won't you, Don?"

"Well, I don't know. I can't afford to run with you fellows with rich fathers."

"O, get out! That don't make any difference," puffed Gus. "The owner of the yacht has to foot the bills. Besides, we want you, Don John, for you know more about a boat than all the rest of the fellows put together."

“Well, I shall be very glad to do anything I can to help the thing along; but there are plenty of fellows that can sail a boat better than I can.”

“But you know all about a boat, and they want you for measurer. We have the printed constitution of a Yacht Club, which Bob Montague got in Boston, and according to that the measurer is entitled to ten cents a foot for measuring a yacht; so you may make something out of your office.”

“I don’t want to make any money out of it,” protested Donald.

“You can make enough to pay your dues, for we have to raise some money for prizes in the regattas; and we talk of having a club house over on Turtle Head,” rattled Gus, whose tongue seemed to be hung on a pivot in his enthusiasm over the club. “Every fellow must be voted in, and pay five dollars a year for membership. We shall have some big times.—We are gaining on the Skylark, as true as you live!”

“I think we are; but I guess Bob isn’t driving her,” added Donald.

“She carries the same sail as the Sea Foam. I would give anything to beat her. Make her do her best, Don John.”

"I will," laughed the skipper, who had kept one eye on the Skylark all the time.

He trimmed the sails a little, and began to be somewhat excited over the prospect of a race. The Christabel was three feet longer than the other yachts, and it was soon evident that in a light wind she was more than a match for them, for she ran ahead of the Sea Foam. Her jib and mainsail were much larger in proportion to her size than those of the other sloops, but she was not an able boat, not a heavy-weather craft, like them. The Sea Foam continued to gain on the Skylark, till she was abreast of her, while the Phantom kept about even with her. But then Robert Montague was busy all the time talking with his companions about the Yacht Club, and did not pay particular attention to the sailing of his boat. The Sea Foam began to walk ahead of him, and then, for the first time, it dawned upon him that the reputation of the Skylark was at stake. He had his crew of five with him, and he placed them in position to improve the sailing of his craft. He ordered one of his hands to give a small pull on the jib-sheet, another to let off the main sheet a little, and a third to haul up the centre-board a little more, as she was going free.

The effect of this attention on the part of the skipper of the Skylark was to lessen the distance between her and the Sea Foam; they were abeam of each other, with the Phantom in the same line. The Christabel was about a cable's length ahead of them.

"She's game yet," said Gus Barker, his disappointment evident in the tones of his voice, as the Skylark came up to the Sea Foam.

"This is a new boat, and I haven't got the hang of her yet," Donald explained. "Haul up that fin a little, Dick."

"What fin?"

"The centre-board."

"Ay, ay," replied Dick, as he obeyed the order.

"Steady! that's enough," continued Donald, who now narrowly watched the sailing of the Sea Foam, to assure himself that she did not make too much leeway.

"That was what she wanted!" exclaimed Gus, when the yacht began to gain again, and in a few minutes was half a length ahead.

"But not quite so much of it," replied Donald,

SEA FOAM

The Start. Page 51.

when he saw that his craft was sliding off a very
little. "Give her just three inches more fin,
Dick."

The centre-board was dropped this distance, and
the tendency to make leeway thus corrected.

"She is gaining still!" cried Gus, delighted.

"Not much; it is a pretty even thing," added
Donald.

"No matter; we beat her, and I don't care if
it's only half an inch in a mile."

"But the Christabel is leading us all. She is
sure of all the first prizes."

"Not a bit of it. She has to reef when there's
a capful of wind In a calm she will beat us, but
when it blows we shall wax her all to pieces."

"Hallo!" shouted Mr. Laud Cavendish, whose
small sail-boat was overhauled about half way
over to Turtle Head. "Is that you, Don John?"

"I believe so," replied Donald.

"Where you going?"

"Over to Turtle Head. Want us to give you
a tow?"

"No; you needn't brag about your old tub.
She don't belong to you; and I'm going to have
a boat that will beat that one all to splinters "
replied Laud.

"All right; fetch her along."

"I say, Don John, I'm going to stop over Sunday on Turtle Head. Won't you stay with me?"

"No, I thank you. I must go home to-night," answered Donald.

Mr. Laud Cavendish knew very well that Donald would not spend Sunday in boating and fishing; and he did not ask because he wanted him. Besides, for more reasons than one, he did not desire his company. The Sea Foam ran out of talking distance of the sail-boat in a moment. Robert Montague was doing his best to keep up the reputation of the Skylark; but when the fleet came up to Turtle Head, she was more than a length behind. The jib was hauled down, the yachts came up into the wind, and the anchors were let go.

"Beat you," shouted Gus Barker.

"Not much," replied Robert. "We will try that over again some time."

"We are willing," added Donald.

The mainsails were lowered, and the young yachtmen embarked in the tenders for the shore. Turtle Head is a rocky point at the northern extremity of Long Island, in Penobscot Bay. There were a few trees near the shore, and under these the party purposed to hold their meeting. Though the weather was intensely hot on shore, it was comfortably cool at the Head, where the wind came over five or six miles of salt water cool from the ocean. The boys leaped ashore, and hauled up their boats where the rising tide could not float them off. There were over twenty of them, all members of the High School.

"The Sea Foam sails well," said Robert Montague, as he walked over to the little grove with Donald.

"Very well, indeed. This is the first time she has been out, and I find she works first rate," replied Donald.

"I want to try it with her some day, when everything is right."

"Wasn't everything right to-day?" asked Donald, smiling, for he was well aware that every boatman has a good excuse for the shortcomings of his craft.

"No; my tender is twice as heavy as yours," added Robert. "I must get your father to build me one like that of the Sea Foam."

"We will try it without any tenders, which we don't want in a race."

"Of course I don't know but the Sea Foam can beat me; but I haven't seen the boat of her inches before that could show her stern to the Skylark," said Robert; and it was plain that he was a little nettled at the slight advantage which the new yacht had gained.

"I should like to sail her when you try it, for I have great hopes of the Sea Foam. If my father has built a boat that will beat the Skylark in all weathers, he has done a big thing, and it will make business good for him."

"For his sake I might be almost willing to be whipped," replied Robert, good-naturedly, as they halted in the grove.

Charley Armstrong was the oldest member of the party, and he was to call the meeting to order, which he did with a brief speech, explaining the object of the gathering, though everybody present knew it perfectly well. Charles was then chosen chairman, and Dick Adams secretary. It was voted to form a club, and the secretary was called upon to read the constitution of the "Dorchester Yacht Club." The name was changed to

Belfast, and the document was adopted as the constitution of the Belfast Yacht Club. The second article declared that the officers should consist of a "Commodore, Vice-Commodore, Captain of the Fleet, Secretary, Treasurer, Measurer, a Board of Trustees, and a Regatta Committee;" and the next business was to elect them, which had to be done by written or printed ballots. As the first three officers were required to be owners in whole, or in part, of yachts enrolled in the club, there was found to be an alarming scarcity of yachts. The Skylark, Sea Foam, Phantom, and Christabel were on hand. Edward Patterdale and Samuel Rodman had signified their intention to join, though they were unable to be present at the first meeting. The Maud, as Samuel Rodman's new yacht was to be called, was to be built at once: she was duly enrolled, thus making a total of five, from whom the first three officers must be chosen.

The secretary had come supplied with stationery, and a slip was handed to each member, after the constitution had been signed. A ballot was taken for commodore; Robert B. Montague had twenty votes, and Charles Armstrong one.

Robert accepted the office in a "neat little speech," and took the chair, which was a sharp rock. Edward Patterdale was elected vice-commodore, and Joseph Guilford captain of the fleet. Donald was chosen measurer, and the other offices filled to the satisfaction of those elected, if not of the others. It was then agreed to have a review and excursion on the following Saturday, to which the ladies were to be invited.

The important business of the day was happily finished, and the fleet sailed for Belfast. Having secured the Sea Foam at her mooring, Donald hastened home. As he approached the cottage, he saw a doctor's sulky at the door, and the neighbors going in and out. His heart rose into his throat, for there was not one living beneath that humble roof whom he did not love better than himself.

CHAPTER IV.

A SAD EVENT IN THE RAMSAY FAMILY.

DONALD'S heart beat violently as he hastened towards the cottage. Before he could reach it, another doctor drew up at the door, and it was painfully certain that one of the family was very sick—dangerously so, or two physicians would not have been summoned. It might be his father, his mother, or his sister Barbara; and whichever it was, it was terrible to think of. His legs almost gave away under him, when he staggered up to the cottage. As he did so, he recalled the fact that his father had been ailing when he went away in the Sea Foam. It must be his father, therefore, who was now so desperately ill as to require the attendance of two doctors.

The cottage was a small affair, with a pretty flower garden in front of it, and a whitewashed fence around it. But small as it was, it was not owned by the boat-builder, who, though not in debt, had hardly anything of this world's goods— possibly a hundred dollars in the savings' bank, and the furniture in the cottage. Though he was as prudent and thrifty as Scotchmen generally are, and was not beset by their "often infirmity," he had not been very prosperous. The business of ship-building had been almost entirely suspended, and for several years only a few small vessels had been built in the city. Ramsay had always obtained work; but he lived well, and gave his daughter and his son an excellent education.

Alexander Ramsay's specialty was the building of yachts and boats, and he determined to make a better use of his skill than selling it with his labor for day wages. He went into business for himself as a boat-builder. When he established himself, he had several hundred dollars, with which he purchased stock and tools. He had built several sail-boats, but the Sea Foam was the largest job he had obtained. Doubtless with life and health he would have done a good business. Donald had always been interested in boats, and he knew the name and shape of every timber and plank in

the hull of a vessel, as well as every spar and
rope. Though only sixteen, he was an excellent
mechanic himself. His father had taken great
pains to instruct him in the use of tools, and in
draughting and modelling boats and larger craft.
He not only studied the art in theory, but he
worked with his own hands. In the parlor of the
little cottage was a full-rigged brig, made entirely
by him. The hull was not a log, shaped and
dug out, but regularly constructed, with timbers
and planking. When he finished it, only a few
months before his introduction to the reader, he
felt competent to build a yacht like the Sea
Foam, without any assistance; but boys are generally over-confident, and possibly he overrated
his ability.

With his heart rising up into his throat, Donald
walked towards the cottage. As he passed the
whitewashed gate, one of the neighbors came out
at the front door. She was an elderly woman,
and she looked very sad as she glanced at the
boy.

"I'm glad you have come, Donald; but I'm
afraid he'll never speak to you again," said she.

"Is it my father?" gasped the poor fellow.

"It is; and he's very sick indeed."

"What ails him?"

"That's more than the doctors can tell yet," added the woman. "They say it's very like the cholera; and I suppose it's cholera-morbus. He has been ailing for several days, and he didn't take care of himself. But go in, Donald, and see him while you may."

The young man entered the cottage. The doctors, his mother and sister, were all doing what they could for the sufferer, who was enduring, with what patience he could, the most agonizing pain. Donald went into the chamber where his father lay writhing upon the bed. The physicians were at work upon him; but he saw his son as he entered the room and held out his hand to him. The boy took it in his own. It was cold and convulsed.

"I'm glad you've come, Donald," groaned he, uttering the words with great difficulty. "Be a good boy always, and take care of your mother and sister."

"I will, father," sobbed Donald, pressing the cold hand he held.

"I was afraid I might never see you again," gasped Mr. Ramsay.

"O, don't give up, my man," said Dr. Wadman. "You may be all right in a few hours."

The sick man said no more. He was in too much pain to speak again, and Dr. Wadman sent Donald to the kitchen for some hot water. When he returned with it he was directed to go to the apothecary's for an ounce of chloroform, which the doctors were using internally and externally, and had exhausted their supply. Donald ran all the way as though the life of his father depended upon his speed. He was absent only a few minutes, but when he came back there was weeping and wailing in the little cottage by the sea-side. His father had breathed his last, even while the doctors were hopefully working to save him.

"O, Donald, Donald!" cried Mrs. Ramsay, as she threw her arms around his neck. "Your poor father is gone!"

The boy could not speak; he could not even weep, though his grief was not less intense than that of his mother and sister. They groaned, and sobbed, and sighed together, till kind neighbors led them from the chamber of death, vainly endeavoring to comfort them. It was hours before they were even tolerably calm; but they could speak of nothing, think of nothing, but him who was gone. The neighbors did all that it was necessary to do, and spent the night with the afflicted ones, who could not separate to seek their beds. The rising sun of the Sabbath found them still up, and still weeping—those who could weep. It was a long, long Sunday to them, and every moment of it was given to him who had been a devoted husband and a tender father. On Monday, all too soon, was the funeral; and all that was mortal of Alexander Ramsay was laid in the silent grave, never more to be looked upon by those who had loved him, and whom he had loved.

The little cottage was like a casket robbed of its single jewel to those who were left. Earth and life seemed like a terrible blank to them. They could not accustom themselves to the empty chair at the window where he sat when his day's work was done; to the vacant place at the table, where he had always invoked the blessing of God on the frugal fare before them; and to the silent and deserted shop on the other side of the street, from which the noise of his hammer and the clip of his adze had come to them. A week wore away and nothing was done but the most necessary offices of the household. The neighbors came frequently to beguile their grief, and the minister made several visits, bearing to them the consolations of the gospel, and the tender message of a genuine sympathy.

But it is not for poor people long to waste themselves in idle lamentations. The problem of the future was forced upon Mrs. Ramsay for solution. If they had been able only to live comfortably on the earnings of the dead husband, what should they do now when the strong arm that delved for them was silent in the cold embrace of death? They must all work now; but even then the poor woman could hardly see how she could keep her family together. Barbara was eighteen, but she had never done anything except to assist her mother, whose health was not very good, about the house. She was a graduate of the High School, and competent, so far as education was concerned, to teach a school if she could obtain a situation. Mrs. Ramsay might obtain work to be done at home, but it was only a pittance she could earn besides doing her housework. She wished to have Donald finish his education at the

High School, but she was afraid this was impossible.

Donald, still mourning for his father, who had
so constantly been his companion in the cottage
and in the shop, that he could not reconcile himself to the loss, hardly thought of the future, till
his mother spoke to him about it. He had often,
since that bitter Saturday night, recalled the last
words his father had ever spoken to him, in which
he had told him to be a good boy always and take
care of his mother and sister; but they had not
much real significance to him till his mother
spoke to him. Then he understood them; then
he saw that his father was conscious of the near
approach of death, and had given his mother and
his sister into his keeping. Then, with the mem-
ory of him who was gone lingering near and dear
in his heart, a mighty resolution was born in his
soul, though it did not at once take a practical
form.

"Don't worry about the future, mother," said
he, after he had listened to her rather hopeless
statement of her views.

"I don't worry about it, Donald, for while we
have our health and strength, we can work and

make a living. I want to keep you in school till the end of the year, but I—''

"Of course I can't go to school any more, mother. I am ready to go to work," interposed Donald.

''I know you are, my boy; but I want you to finish your school course very much.''

''I haven't thought a great deal about the matter yet, mother, but I think I shall be able to do what father told me.''

''Your father did not expect you to take care of us till you had grown up, I'm sure,'' added Mrs. Ramsay, who had heard the dying injunction of her husband to their son.

''I don't know that he did; but I shall do the best I can.''

''Poor father! He never thought of anything but us,'' sighed Mrs. Ramsay; and her woman's tears flowed freely again, so freely that there was no power of utterance left to her.

Donald wept, too, as he thought of him who was not only his father, but his loving companion in study, in work, and in play. He left the house and walked over to the shop. For the first time since the sad event, he unlocked the door

and entered. The tears trickled down his cheeks
as he glanced at the bench where his father had
done his last day's work. The planes and a few
other tools were neatly arranged upon it, and his
apron was spread over them. On the walls were
models of boats and yachts, and in one corner
were the "moulds." Donald seated himself on
the tool-chest, and looked around at every familiar object in the shop. He was thinking of something, but his thought had not yet taken definite
form. While he was considering the present and
the future, Samuel Rodman entered the shop.

"Do you suppose I can get the model of the
Sea Foam, Don John?" inquired he, after something had been said about the deceased boat-
builder.

"I think you can. The model and the drawings are all here," replied Donald.

"We intend to build the Maud this season, and
I want her to be as near like the Sea Foam as possible."

"Who is going to build her?" asked Donald,
his interest suddenly kindled by the question.

"I don't know; we haven't spoken to any one
about it yet," replied Samuel. "There isn't any-

Don John wants a Job. Page 73.

body in these parts that can build her as your father would.”

“Sam, can’t I do this job for you?” said Donald.

“You?”

“Yes, I. You know I used to work with my father, and I understand his way of doing things.”

“Well, I hadn’t thought that you could do it; but I will talk with my father about it,” answered Samuel, who appeared to have some doubts about the ability of his friend to do so large a job.

“I don’t mean to do it all myself, Sam. I will hire one or two first-rate ship carpenters,” added Donald. “She shall be just like the Sea Foam, except a little alteration, which my father explained to me, in the bow and run.”

“Do you think you could do the job, Don John?” asked Samuel, with an incredulous smile.

“I know I could,” said Donald, earnestly. “If I had time enough I could build her all alone.”

“We want her as soon as we can get her.”

“She shall be finished as quick as my father could have done her.”

"I will see my father about it to-night, Don John, and let you know to-morrow. I came down to see about the model."

Samuel Rodman left the shop and walked down the beach to the sail-boat in which he had come. Donald was almost inspired by the idea which had taken possession of him. If he could only carry on his father's business, he could make money enough to support the family; and knowing every stick in the hull of a vessel, he felt competent to do so. Full of enthusiasm, he hastened into the cottage to unfold his brilliant scheme to his mother. He stated his plan to her, but at first she shook her head.

"Do you think you could build a yacht, Donald?" she asked.

"I am certain I could. Didn't you hear father say that my brig contained every timber and plank that belongs to a vessel?"

"Yes, and that the work was done as well as he could do it himself; but that does not prove that you can carry on the business."

"I want one or two men, if we build the Maud, because it would take too long for me to do all the work alone."

"The Maud?"

"That was the yacht that father was to build next. I asked Sam Rodman to give me the job, and he is going to talk with his father about it to-night."

Mrs. Ramsay was rather startled at this announcement, which indicated that her son really meant business in earnest.

"Do you think he will let you do it?" she asked.

"I hope he will."

"Are you sure you can make anything if you build the yacht?"

"Father made over three hundred dollars on the Sea Foam, besides his day wages."

"That is no reason why you can do it."

"All his models, moulds, and draughts are in the shop. I know where they are, and just what to do with them. I hope you will let me try it, mother."

"Suppose you don't make out?"

"But I shall make out."

"If Mr. Rodman refuses to accept the yacht after the job is done, what will you do?"

"I shall have her myself then, and I can make lots of money taking out parties in her."

"Your father was paid for the Sea Foam as the work progressed. He had received eight hundred dollars on her when she was finished."

"I know it; and Captain Patterdale owes four hundred more. If you let me use some of the money to buy stock and pay the men till I get payment on the job, I shall do very well."

"We must have something to live on. After I have paid the funeral expenses and other bills, this money that Captain Patterdale owes will be all I have."

"But Mr. Rodman will pay me something on the job, when he is satisfied that the work will be done."

The widow was not very clear about the business; but she concluded, at last, that if Mr. Rodman would give him the job, she would allow him to undertake it. Donald was satisfied, and went back to the shop. He opened his father's chest and took out his account book. Turning to a page which was headed "Sea Foam," he found every item of labor and expenditure charged to her. Every day's work, every foot of stock, every pound of nails, every article of brass or hardware, and the cost of sails and cordage, were carefully entered on the account. From this he could learn the price of everything used in the construction of the yacht, for his guidance in the great undertaking before him. But he was quite familiar before with the cost of everything used in building a boat. On a piece of smooth board, he figured up the probable cost, and assured himself he could make a good job of the building of the Maud.

The next day was Saturday—two weeks after the organization of the yacht club. There had been a grand review a week before, which Donald did not attend. The yachtmen had taken their mothers, sisters, and other friends on an excursion down the bay, and given them a collation at Turtle Head. On the Saturday in question, a meeting of the club at the Head had been called to complete the arrangements for a regatta, and the Committee on Regattas were to make their report. Donald had been requested to attend in order to measure the yachts. He did not feel much like taking part in the sports of the club, but he decided to perform the duty required of him. He expected to see Samuel Rodman on this occasion, and to learn the decision of his father in regard to the building of the Maud.

After breakfast he embarked in the sail-boat which had belonged to his father, and with a fresh breeze stood over to Turtle Head. He had dug some clams early in the morning, and told his mother he should bring home some fish which he intended to catch after the meeting of the club. As the boat sped on her way, he thought of his grand scheme to carry on his father's business, and everything seemed to depend upon Mr. Rodman's decision. He hoped for the best, but he trembled for the result. When he reached his destination, he found another boat at the Head, and soon discovered Laud Cavendish on the bluff.

"Hallo, Don John!" shouted the swell, as Donald stepped on shore.

"How are you, Laud? You are out early."

"Not very; I came ashore here to see if I couldn't find some clams," added Laud, as he held up a clam-digger he carried in his hand—a kind of trowel fixed in a shovel-handle.

"You can't find any clams here," said Donald, wondering that even such a swell should expect to find them there.

"I am going down to Camden to stay over Sunday, and I thought I might fish a little on the way."

"You will find some farther down the shore, where there is a soft beach. Do you get off every Saturday now, Laud?"

"Get off? Yes; I get off every day. I'm out of a job."

"I thought you were at Miller's store."

"I was there; but I'm not now. Miller shoved me out. Do you know of any fellow that has a good boat to sell?"

"What kind of a boat?"

"Well, one like the Skylark and the Sea Foam."

"No; I don't know of any one around here. Do you want to buy one?"

"Yes; I thought I would buy one, if I could get her about right. She must be cheap."

"How cheap do you expect to buy a boat like the Sea Foam?" asked Donald, wondering what a young man out of business could be thinking about when he talked of buying a yacht.

"Four or five hundred dollars."

"The Sea Foam cost twelve hundred."

"That's a fancy price. The Skylark didn't cost but five hundred."

"Do you want to give five hundred for a boat?"

"Not for myself, Don John. I was going to buy one for another man. I must be going now," added Laud, as he went down to his boat.

Hoisting his sail, he shoved off, and stood over towards Scarsport. Donald walked up the slope to the Head, from which he could see the yacht club fleet as soon as it sailed from the city.

CHAPTER V.

CAPTAIN SHIVERNOCK.

DONALD seated himself on a rock, with his gaze directed towards Belfast. His particular desire just then was to see Samuel Rodman, in order to learn whether he was to have the job of building the Maud. He felt able to do it, and even then, as he thought of the work, he had in his mind the symmetrical lines of the new yacht, as they were to be after the change in the model which his father had explained to him. He recalled a suggestion of a small increase in the size of the mainsail, which had occurred to him when he sailed the Sea Foam. His first aspiration was only to build a yacht; his second was to build one that would beat anything of her inches in the fleet. If he could realize this last ambition, he would have all the business he could do.

The yacht fleet did not appear up the bay; but

it was only nine o'clock in the morning, and possibly the meeting of the club would not take place till afternoon. If any one had told him the hour, he had forgotten it, but the former meeting had been in the forenoon. He was too nervous to sit still a great while, and, rising, he walked about, musing upon his grand scheme. The place was an elevated platform of rock, a portion of it covered with soil to the depth of several feet, on which the grass grew. It was not far above the water even at high tide, nor were the bluffs very bold. The plateau was on a peninsula, extending to the north from the island, which was not unlike the head of a turtle, and the shape had given it a name. Donald walked back and forth on the headland, watching for the fleet.

"I wonder if Laud Cavendish was digging for clams up here," thought he, as he observed a spot where the earth appeared to have been disturbed.

The marks of Laud's clam-digger were plainly to be seen in the loam, a small quantity of which remained on the sod. Certainly the swell had been digging there; but it could not have been for clams; and Donald was trying to imagine what it was for, when he heard footsteps near him. Coming towards him, he discovered Captain Shivernock, of the city; and he had two problems to solve instead of one; not very important ones, it is true, but just such as are suggested to everybody at times. Perhaps it did not make the least difference to the young man whether or not he ascertained why Laud Cavendish had been digging on the Head, or why Captain Shivernock happened to be on the island, apparently without any boat, at that time in the morning. I do not think Donald would have given a nickel five-cent piece to have been informed correctly upon either point, though he did propose the question to himself in each case. Probably Laud had no particular object in view in digging—the ground did not look as though he had; and Captain Shivernock was odd enough to do anything, or to be anywhere, at the most unseasonable hours.

"How are you, Don John?" shouted the captain, as he came within hailing distance of Donald.

"How do you do, Captain Shivernock," replied the young man, rather coldly, for he had no regard, and certainly no admiration, for the man.

"You are just the man I wanted to see," added the captain.

Donald could not reciprocate the sentiment, and, not being a hypocrite, he made no reply. The captain seemed to be somewhat fatigued and out of breath, and immediately seated himself on the flat rock which the young man had occupied. He was not more than five feet and a half high, but was tolerably stout. The top of his head was as bald as a winter squash; but extending around the back of his head from ear to ear was a heavy fringe of red hair. His whiskers were of the same color; but, as age began to bleach them out under the chin, he shaved this portion of his figure-head, while his side whiskers and mustache were very long. He was dressed in a complete suit of gray, and wore a coarse braided straw hat.

Captain Shivernock, as I have more than once hinted, was an eccentric man. He had been a shipmaster in the earlier years of his life, and had made a fortune by some lucky speculations during the War of the Rebellion, in which he took counsel of his interest rather than his patriotism. He had a strong will, a violent temper, and an implacable hatred to any man who had done him an injury, either actually or constructively. It was said that he was as faithful and devoted in his friendships as he was bitter and relentless in his hatreds; but no one in the city, where he was a very unpopular man, had any particular experience of the soft side of his character. He was a native of Lincolnville, near Belfast, though he had left his home in his youth. He had a fine house in the city, and lived in good style. He was said to be a widower, and had no children. The husband of his housekeeper was the man of all work about his place, and both of them had come with their employer from New York.

He seldom did anything like other people. He never went to church, would never put his name upon a subscription paper, however worthy the object, though he had been known to give a poor man an extravagant reward for a slight service. He would not pay his taxes till the fangs of the law worried the money out of him, but would give fifty dollars for the first salmon or the first dish of peaches of the season for his table. He was as full of contradictions as he was of oddities, and no one knew how to take him. One moment he seemed to be hoarding his money like a miser, and the next scattering it with insane prodigality.

"I'm tired out, Don John," added Captain Shivernock, as he seated himself, fanning his red face with his hat.

"Have you walked far, sir?" asked Donald, who was well acquainted with the captain; for his father had worked on his boat, and he was often in the shop.

"I believe I have hoofed it about ten miles this morning," replied Captain Shivernock with an oath; and he had a wicked habit of ornamenting every sentence he used with a profane expletive, which I shall invariably omit.

"Then you have walked nearly the whole length of the island."

"Do you mean to tell me I lie?" demanded the captain.

"Certainly not, sir," protested Donald.

"My boat got aground down here. I started early this morning to go down to Vinal Haven; but I'm dished now, and can't go," continued Captain Shivernock, so interlarding with oaths this simple statement that it looks like another thing divested of them.

"Where did you get aground?" asked Donald.

"Down by Seal Harbor."

"About three miles from here."

"Do you think I lied to you?"

"By no means, sir."

Donald could not divine how the captain had got aground near Seal Harbor, if he was bound from Belfast to Vinal Haven, though it was possible that the wind had been more to the southward early in the morning, compelling him to beat down the bay; but it was not prudent to question anything the captain said.

"I ran in shore pretty well, and took the ground. I tried for half an hour to get the Juno off, but I was soon left high and dry on the beach. I anchored her where she was, and I'm sorry now I didn't set her afire," explained the captain.

"Set her afire!" exclaimed Donald.

"That's what I said. She shall never play me such a trick again," growled the strange man.

"Why, it wasn't the fault of the boat."

"Do you mean to say it was my fault?" de-

manded the captain, ripping out a string of oaths
that made Donald shiver.

"It was an accident which might happen to any
one."

"Do you think I didn't know what I was
about?"

"I suppose you did, sir; but any boat may get
aground."

"Not with me! if she did I'd burn her or sell
her for old junk. I never will sail in her again
after I get home. I know what I'm about."

"Of course you do, sir."

"Got a boat here?" suddenly demanded the
eccentric.

"Yes, sir; I have our sail-boat."

"Take me down to Seal Harbor in her," added
the captain, rising from his seat.

"I don't think I can go, sir."

"Don't you? What's the reason you can't?"
asked the captain, with a sneer on his lips.

"I have to meet the yacht club here."

Captain Shivernock cursed the yacht club with
decided unction, and insisted that Donald should
convey him in his boat to the place where the
Juno was at anchor.

"I have to measure the yachts when they come, sir."

"Measure—" but the place the captain suggested was not capable of measurement. "I'll pay you well for going."

"I should not ask any pay if I could go," added Donald, glancing up the bay to see if the fleet was under way.

"I say I will pay you well, and you will be a fool if you don't go with me."

"The yachts haven't started yet, and perhaps I shall have time to get back before they arrive."

"I don't care whether you get back or not; I want you to go."

"I will go, sir, and run the risk," replied Donald, as he led the way down to the boat.

Shoving her off, he helped the captain into her, and hoisted the sail.

"What boat's that over there?" demanded Captain Shivernock, as he pointed at the craft sailed by Laud Cavendish, which was still standing on towards Searsport.

Donald told him who was in her.

"Don't go near her," said he, sternly. "I always want a good mile between me and that puppy."

"He is bound to Camden, and won't get there for a week at that rate," added Donald.

"Don't care if he don't," growled the passenger.

"I don't know that I do, either," added the skipper. "Laud wants to buy a boat, and perhaps you can sell him yours, if you are tired of her."

"Shut up!"

Donald did "shut up," and decided not to make any more talk with the captain, only to give him civil answers. Ordinarily he would as soon have thought of wrestling with a Bengal tiger as of carrying on a conversation with such a porcupine as his passenger, who scrupled not to insult man or boy without the slightest provocation. In a few moments the skipper tacked, having weathered the Head, and stood into the little bay west of it.

"Don John," said Captain Shivernock, sharply, fixing his gaze upon the skipper.

"Sir?"

The captain took his wallet from his pocket. It was well filled with greenbacks, from which he took several ten-dollar bills—five or six of them, at least.

"I will pay you," said he.

"I don't ask any pay for this, sir. I am willing to do you a favor for nothing."

"Hold your tongue, you fool! A favor?" sneered the eccentric. "Do you think I would ask a little monkey like you to do me a favor?"

"I won't call it a favor, sir."

"Better not. There! take that," and Captain Shivernock shoved the bills he had taken from his wallet into Donald's hand.

"No, sir! I can't take all that, if I do anything," protested the skipper, amazed at the generosity of his passenger. The captain, with a sudden spring, grasped a short boat-hook which lay between the rail and the wash-board.

"Put that money into your pocket, or I'll smash your head; and you won't be the first man I've killed, either," said the violent passenger.

Donald did not find the money hard to take on its own merits, and he considerately obeyed the savage order. His pride, which revolted at the idea of being paid for a slight service rendered to a neighbor, was effectually conquered. He put the money in his pocket; but as soon as

the captain laid down the boat-hook, he took it
out to count it, and found there was fifty dollars. He deposited it carefully in his wallet.

"You don't mean to pay me all that money for
this little job?" said he.

"Do you think I don't know what I mean?"
snarled the passenger.

"I suppose you do, sir."

"You suppose I do!" sneered the cynic. "You
know I do."

"Fifty dollars is a great deal of money for
such a little job."

"That's none of your business. Don John,
you've got a tongue in your head!" said Captain Shivernock, pointing his finger at the skipper, and glowering upon him as though he was
charging him with some heinous crime.

"I am aware of it, sir," replied Donald.

"Do you know what a tongue is for?" demanded the captain.

"It is of great assistance to one in talking."

"Don't equivocate, you sick monkey. Do
you know what a tongue is for?"

"Yes, sir."

"What's a tongue for?"

"To talk with, and—"

"That's enough! I thought you would say so. You are an ignorant whelp."

"Isn't the tongue to talk with?"

"No!" roared the passenger.

"What is it for, then?" asked Donald, who did not know whether to be alarmed or amused at the manner of his violent companion.

"It's to keep still with, you canting little monkey! And that's what I want you to do with your tongue," replied Captain Shivernock.

"I don't think I understand you, sir."

"I don't think you do. How could you, when I haven't told you what I mean. Listen to me."

The eccentric paused, and fixed his gaze earnestly upon the skipper.

"Have you seen me this morning?" demanded he.

"Of course I have."

"No, you haven't!"

"I really thought I had."

"Thought's a fool, and you're another! You haven't seen me. If anybody in Belfast asks you if you have seen me, tell 'em you haven't."

"If the tongue isn't to talk with, it isn't to tell a lie with," added Donald.

"Ha, ha, ha!" laughed the captain; "you've got me there."

He produced his wallet again, and took a ten-dollar bill from the roll it contained, which he tendered to Donald.

"What's that for?" asked the skipper.

"Put it in your pocket, or I'll mash your empty skull!"

Donald placed it with the other bills in his wallet, more than ever amazed at the conduct of his singular passenger.

"I never allow anyone to get ahead of me without paying for my own stupidity. Do you go to Sunday School, and church, and missionary meetings?" asked the captain, with a sneer.

"I do, sir."

"I thought so. You are a sick monkey. You don't let your tongue tell a lie."

"No, sir; I don't mean to tell a lie, if I can help it, and I generally can."

"You walk in the strait and narrow way which leads to the meeting-house. I don't. All right! Broad is the way! But one thing is certain, Don John, you haven't seen me to-day."

"But I have," persisted Donald.

"I say you have not; don't contradict me, if you want to take that head of yours home with you. Nobody will ask whether you have seen me or not; so that if a lie is likely to choke you, keep still with your tongue."

"I am not to say that I have seen you on the island?" queried Donald.

"You are not," replied the captain, with an echoing expletive.

"Why not, sir?"

"None of your business! Do as you are told, and spend the money I gave you for gingerbread and fast horses."

"But when my mother sees this money she will want to know where I got it."

"If you tell her or anybody else, I'll hammer your head till it isn't thicker than a piece of sheet-iron. Don't let her see the money. Hire a fast horse, and go to ride next Sunday."

"I don't go to ride on Sunday."

"I suppose not. Give it to the missionaries to buy red flannel shirts for little niggers in the West Indies, if you like. I don't care what you do with it."

"You don't wish anybody to know you have

been on the island this morning—is that the idea,
Captain Shivernock?" asked Donald, not a little
alarmed at the position in which his companion
was placing him.

"That's the idea, Don John."

"I don't see why—"

"You are not to see why," interrupted the captain, fiercely. "That's my business, not yours.
Will you do as I tell you?"

"If there is any trouble—"

"There isn't any trouble. Do you think I've
killed somebody?—No. Do you think I've
robbed somebody?—No. Do you think I've set
somebody's house on fire?—No. Do you think
I've stolen somebody's chickens?—No. Nothing
of the sort. I want to know whether you can
keep your tongue still. Let us see. There's
the Juno."

"Somebody will see your boat, and know that
you have been here—"

"That's my business, not yours. Don't bother
your head with what don't concern you," growled
the passenger.

The Juno was afloat, but she could not have
been so many minutes, when Donald came along-

side of her. It was now about half tide on the
flood, and she must have grounded at about half
tide on the ebb. This fact indicated that Captain
Shivernock had left her at four o’clock in the
morning. The owner of the Juno stepped into
her, and Donald hoisted the sail for him. The
boat was cat-rigged, and about twenty-four feet
long. She was a fine craft, with a small cabin
forward, furnished with every convenience the
limited space would permit. The captain seated
himself in the standing-room, and began to heap
maledictions upon the boat.

“I never will sail in her again,” said he. “I
will burn her, and get a centre-board boat.”

“What will you take for her, sir?” asked
Donald.

“Do you want her, Don John?” demanded the
captain.

“I couldn’t afford to keep her; but I will sell
her for you.”

“Sell—” it is no matter what; but Captain Shivernock suddenly leaped back into Donald’s boat,
and her skipper wondered what he intended to do
next. “She is yours, Don John!” he exclaimed.

“To sell for you?”

7

"No! Sell her, if you like, but put the money in your own pocket. I will sail up in your boat, and you may go to Jerusalem in the Juno, if you like. I will never get into her again," added the captain, spitefully.

"But, Captain Shivernock, you surely don't mean to *give* me this boat."

"Do you think I don't know what I mean?" roared the strange man, after a long string of expletives. "She is yours, now; not mine. I'll give you a bill of sale as soon as I go ashore. Not another word, or I'll pound your head. Don't tell anybody I gave her to you, or that you have seen me. If you do there will be a job for a coffin-maker."

The captain shoved off the boat, and laid her course across the bay, evidently to avoid Laud Cavendish, whose craft was a mile distant; for he had probably put in at Searsport. Donald weighed the anchor of the Juno, and sailed for Turtle Head, hardly knowing whether he was himself or somebody else, so amazed was he at the strange conduct of his late passenger. He could not begin to comprehend it, and he did not have to strain his logic very much in coming to the conclusion that the captain was insane.

CHAPTER VI.

DONALD GETS THE JOB.

WHETHER Captain Shivernock was sane or insane, Donald Ramsay was in possession of the Juno. Of course he did not consider himself the proprietor of the craft, if he did of the sixty dollars he had in his pocket. She had the wind over her port quarter, and the boat tore through the water as if she intended to show her new skipper what she could do. But Donald paid little attention to the speed of the Juno, for his attention was wholly absorbed by the remarkable events of the morning. Captain Shivernock had given him sixty dollars in payment nominally for the slight service rendered him. But then, the strange man had given a poor laborer a hundred dollars for stopping his horse, when the animal leisurely walked towards home from the store where the owner had left him. Again, he had given a negro sailor a fifty-dollar bill for sculling him across the river. He had rewarded a small boy with a ten-dollar bill for bringing him a despatch from the telegraph office. When the woman who went to his house to do the washing was taken sick, and was not able to work for three months, he regularly called at her rooms every Monday morning and gave her ten dollars, which was three times as much as she ever earned in the same time.

Remembering these instances of the captain's bounty, Donald had no doubt about the ownership of the sixty dollars in his pocket. The money was his own; but how had he earned it? Was he paid to keep his tongue still, or simply for the service performed? If for his silence, what had the captain done which made him desire to conceal the fact that he had been to the island? The strange man had explicitly denied having killed, robbed, or stolen from anybody. All the skipper could make of it was, that his desire for silence was only a whim of the captain, and he was entirely willing to accommodate him. If there had been any mischief done on the island, he should hear of it; and in that event he would take counsel of some one older and wiser than himself. Then he tried to satisfy himself as to why the captain had walked at least three miles to Turtle Head, instead of waiting till the tide floated the Juno. This appeared to be also a whim of the strange man. People in the city used to say it was no use to ask the reason for anything that Captain Shivernock did. His motive in giving Donald sixty dollars and his boat, which would sell readily for three hundred dollars, and had cost over five hundred, was utterly unaccountable.

Donald was determined not to do anything wrong, and if the captain had committed any evil deed, he fully intended to expose him; but he meant to keep still until he learned that the evil deed had been done. The money in his pocket, and that for which the Juno could be sold, would be capital enough to enable him to carry on the business of boat-building. But he was determined to see Captain Shivernock that very day in regard to the boat. Perhaps the strange man would give him a job to build a centre-board yacht, for he wanted one.

"Hallo! Juno, ahoy!" shouted Laud Cavendish.

Donald threw the boat up into the wind, under the stern of Laud's craft.

"I thought you were going down to Camden," said he. "You won't get there to-day at this rate."

"I forgot some things I wanted, and ran up to Searsport after them. But what are you doing in the Juno, Don John?"

"She's going to be sold, Laud," replied Donald, dodging the direct question. "Didn't you say you wanted to buy a boat?"

"I said so; and I want to buy one badly. I'm going to spend my summer on the water. What does the captain ask for her?"

"I don't know what the price is, but I'll let you know on Monday," added Donald, as he filled away again, for the yacht fleet was now in sight.

"Hold on a minute, Don John; I want to talk with you about her."

"I can't stop now. I have to go up to the Head and measure the yachts."

"Don't say a word to anybody about my buying her," added Laud.

He was soon out of hearing of Laud's voice. He wondered if the swell really wished to buy such a boat as the Juno, and could pay three hundred dollars for her. His father was not a rich man, and he was out of business himself. And he wanted Donald to keep still too. What motive had he for wishing his proposition to be kept in the dark? His object was not apparent, and Donald was obliged to give up the conundrum, though he had some painful doubts on the subject. As he thought of the matter, he turned to observe the position of the two boats to the southward of him. Directly ahead of Laud's craft was an island which he could not weather, and he was obliged to tack. He could not lay his course, and he had to take a short and then a long stretch, and he was now standing across the bay on the short leg. Captain Shivernock had run over towards the Northport shore, and Donald thought they could not well avoid coming within hailing distance of each other. But the Juno passed beyond the north-west point of the island, and he could no longer see them. He concluded, however, that the captain would not let Laud, or any one else, see him afloat that day. He was a very strange man.

Donald ran the Juno around the point, and

anchored her under the lee of Turtle Head. The
fleet was still a couple of miles distant, and after
he had lowered and secured the mainsail, he had
nothing to do but examine the fine craft which
had so strangely come into his possession. He
went into the cuddy forward, and overhauled
everything there, till he was fully qualified to set
forth the merits of her accommodations to a purchaser. The survey was calculated to kindle his
own enthusiasm, for Donald was as fond of boating as any young man in the club. The idea of
keeping the Juno for his own use occurred to
him, but he resisted the temptation, and determined not even to think of such an extravagant
plan.

The yacht fleet was now approaching, the Skylark gallantly leading the way, and the Christabel, with a reef in her mainsail, bringing up the
rear. The Sea Foam did not seem to hold her
own with the Skylark, as she had done before,
but she was the second to drop her anchor
under the lee of Turtle Head.

"I am glad to see you, Don John," said
Commodore Montague, as he discovered Donald
in the Juno. "I was afraid you were not com-

ing, and I went up to the shop to look for you. But how came you in that boat?"

"She is for sale," replied Donald, as the tender of the Skylark came alongside the Juno, and he stepped into it. "Do you know of anybody that wants to buy her?"

"I know three or four who want boats, but I am not sure the Juno would suit either of them," replied the commodore.

The boat pulled to the shore, and no one asked any more questions about the Juno, or her late owner. The members of the club on board of the several yachts landed, and Donald was soon in earnest conversation with Samuel Rodman.

"What does your father say?" he asked.

"He wants to see you," replied Samuel.

"Does he think I can't do the job?"

"He did not think so at first, but when I told him you would employ one or two regular ship carpenters, he was satisfied, and I think he will give you the job."

"I hope he will, and I am sure I can give him as good work as he can get anywhere."

"I haven't any doubt of it, Don John. But the Sea Foam isn't doing so well as she did the first day you had her out. The Skylark beats her every time they sail.”

“Ned Patterdale hasn’t got the hang of her yet.”

“Perhaps not.”

“I should like to have Bob Montague sail her, and Ned the Skylark; I think it would make a difference,” added Donald. “Ned does very well, but a skipper must get used to his boat; and he hasn’t had much experience in yachts as large as the Sea Foam. I spoke to you of a change in the model for the Maud; and if I’m not greatly mistaken, she will beat both the Sea Foam and the Skylark.”

“I would give all my spending-money for a year, over and above the cost, if she would do that,” replied Rodman, with a snap of the eye.

“Of course I can’t promise that she will do it, but I expect she will,” said Donald.

The club assembled under the trees, and the members were called to order by the commodore. The first business was to hear the report of the Regatta Committee, which proved to be a very interesting document to the yachtmen. The race was to take place the next Saturday, and was open to all yachts exceeding twenty feet in length, duly entered before the time. All were to sail in the same class; the first prize was a silver vase, and the second a marine glass. The course was to be from the judge's boat, in Belfast harbor, by Turtle Head, around the buoy on Stubb's Point Ledge, leaving it on the port hand, and back to the starting-point. The sailing regulations already adopted by the club were to be in full force. The report was accepted, and the members looked forward with eager anticipation to what they regarded as the greatest event of the season. Other business was transacted, and Donald, who had brought with him a measuring tape and plummet, measured all the yachts of the club. Dinner was served on board of each craft, and the commodore extended the hospitalities of the Skylark to Donald.

In the afternoon, the fleet made an excursion around Long Island, returning to Belfast about six o'clock, Donald sailing the Juno, and catching a mess of fish off Haddock Ledge. He moored her off the shop, and was rather surprised to find that his own boat had not yet been returned. After supper he hastened to the house of Mr. Rodman, with whom he had a long talk in regard to the building of the Maud. The gentleman had some doubts about the ability of the young boat-builder to do so large a job, though he desired to encourage him.

"I am willing to give you the work, and to pay you the same price your father had for the Sea Foam; but I don't like to pay out money till I know that you are to succeed," said he.

"I don't ask you to do so, sir," replied Donald, warmly. "You need not pay me a cent till you are perfectly satisfied."

"But I supposed you would want money to buy stock and pay your men, even before you had set up your frame."

"No, sir; we have capital enough to make a beginning."

"I am satisfied then, and you shall have the job," added Mr. Rodman.

"Thank you, sir," replied Donald, delighted at his success.

"You may go to work as soon as you please; and the sooner the better, for Samuel is in a great hurry for his yacht."

"I will go to work on Monday morning. The

model, moulds, and drawings are all ready, and there will be no delay, sir," answered the young boat-builder, as he took his leave of his considerate patron.

Perhaps Mr. Rodman was not satisfied that the young man would succeed in the undertaking, but he had not the heart to discourage one who was so earnest. He determined to watch the progress of the work very closely, and if he discovered that the enterprise was not likely to be successful, he intended to stop it before much time or money had been wasted. Donald had fully detailed the means at his command for doing the job in a workman-like manner, and he was well known as an ingenious and skilful mechanic. Mr. Rodman had strong hopes that the young man would succeed in his undertaking.

Donald walked toward the house of Captain Shivernock, congratulating himself on the happy issue of his interview with Mr. Rodman. As he passed the book and periodical store, he saw Lawrence Kennedy, a ship carpenter, who had formerly worked with Mr. Ramsay, standing at the door, reading the weekly paper just from the press. This man was out of work, and was talk-

ing of going to Bath to find employment. Donald had already thought of him as one of his
hands, for Kennedy was a capital mechanic.

"What's the news?" asked Donald, rather to
open the way to what he had to say, than because
he was interested in the latest intelligence.

"How are you, Donald?" replied the ship
carpenter. "There's a bit of news from Lincolnville, but I suppose you heard it; for all the town
is talking about it."

"I haven't heard it."

"A man in Lincolnville was taken from his
bed in the dead hour of the night, and beaten to
a jelly."

"Who was the man?"

"His name was Hasbrook."

"Hasbrook!" exclaimed Donald.

"Do you know him, lad?"

"I know of him; and he has the reputation of
being anything but an honest man."

"Then it's not much matter," laughed the ship
carpenter.

"But who beat him?" asked Donald.

"No one knows who it was. Hasbrook
couldn't make him out; but likely it's some one
the rogue has cheated."

"Hasbrook must have seen him," suggested Donald.

"The ruffian was disguised with his head in a bit of a bag, or something of that sort, and he never spoke a word from first to last," added Kennedy, looking over the article in the paper.

Donald wondered if Captain Shivernock had any dealings with Hasbrook. He was just the man to take the law into his own hands, and assault one who had done him a real or a fancied injury. Donald began to think he understood why the captain did not wish it to be known that he was on Long Island the night before. But the outrage had been committed in Lincolnville, which bordered the western arm of Penobscot Bay. It was three miles from the main land to the island. If the captain was in Lincolnville in "the dead of night," on a criminal errand, what was he doing near Seal Harbor, where the Juno was aground, at four o'clock in the morning? If he was the guilty party, he would naturally desire to get home before daylight. The wind was fair for him to do so, and there was enough of it to enable the Juno to make the run in less than two hours. It did not seem probable, therefore, that the captain had gone over to the other side of the bay, three miles off his course. Besides, he was not disguised, but wore his usual gray suit; and Hasbrook ought to have been able to recognize him by his form and his dress even in the darkest night.

Donald was perplexed and disturbed. If there was any probability that Captain Shivernock had committed the crime, our hero was not to be bribed by sixty or six thousand dollars to keep the secret. If guilty, he would have been more likely to go below and turn in than to walk three miles on the island for assistance, and he would not have gone three miles off his course. But Donald determined to inquire into the matter, and do his whole duty, even if the strange man killed him for it. Kennedy was reading his paper while the young man was thinking over the case; but, having decided what to do, he interrupted the ship carpenter again.

"Are you still out of work, Mr. Kennedy?" he asked.

"I am; and I think I shall go to Bath next week," replied Kennedy.

"I know of a job for you."

The News from Linconville. Page 110.

"Do you, lad? I don't want to move away from Belfast, and I should be glad to get work here. What's the job?"

"We are going to build a yacht of the size of the Sea Foam."

"Who?" inquired the workman.

"My mother and I intend to carry on my father's business."

"And you wish me to manage it for you?"

"No; I intend to manage it myself," added Donald, confidently.

"Well, lad, you are clever enough to do it; and if you are like your father, I shall be glad to work for you."

The wages were agreed upon, and Kennedy promised to be at the shop on Monday morning, to assist the young boat-builder in selecting the stock for the Maud. Donald walked to the house of Captain Shivernock. In the yard he found Sykes, the man who did all sorts of work for his employer, from taking care of the horses up to negotiating mortgages. Donald had occasionally been to the house, and he knew Sykes well enough to pass the time of day with him when they met in the street.

"Is Captain Shivernock at home?" asked the young man, trying to appear indifferent, for he wanted to get as much information in regard to the strange man's movements during the last twenty-four hours as possible.

"No, he is not," replied Sykes, who to some extent aped the manners of his eccentric employer.

"Not at home!" exclaimed Donald, who had not expected this answer, though he had not found his own boat at her moorings on his return from the excursion with the fleet.

"Are you deaf, young man?"

"No, sir; not at all."

"Then you heard me say he was not at home," growled Sykes.

"I want to see him very much. Will he be long away?" asked Donald.

"I can't tell you. He won't come back till he gets ready, if it isn't for a month."

"Of course not; but I should like to know when I can probably see him."

"You can probably see him when he comes home. He started in his boat for Vinal Haven early this morning."

"This morning?" repeated Donald, who wished to be sure on this point.

"Didn't I say so? This morning. He comes back when he pleases."

"When do you expect him?"

"I don't expect him. I never expect him. He may be home in five minutes, in five days, or five weeks."

"At what time this morning did he go?"

"He left the house at five minutes after four this morning, the last that ever was. I looked at my watch when he went out at the gate; for I was thinking whether or no his boat wasn't aground. Do you want to know what he had for breakfast? If you do, you must ask my wife, for I don't know," growled Sykes.

"I am very anxious to see him," continued Donald, without heeding the sulky tones and manner of the man. "Perhaps he told Mrs. Sykes when he should return."

"Perhaps he did, and perhaps he told her how much money he had in his pocket. He was as likely to tell her one as the other. You can ask her," sneered Sykes.

As the housekeeper sat on the piazza enjoying the cool evening breeze, Donald decided to avail himself of this permission, for he desired to know how well the two stories would agree. He saluted the lady, who gave him a pleasanter reception than her bearish husband had accorded to him.

"Mr. Sykes told me that Captain Shivernock was away from home," said Donald. "Can you tell me when he is likely to return?"

"He intended to come back to-night if the wind favored him. He went to Vinal Haven early this morning, and as you are a sailor, you can tell better than I whether he is likely to return to-night," replied Mrs. Sykes.

"The wind is fair, and there is plenty of it," added Donald. "What time did he leave?"

"About four o'clock. I gave him his coffee at half past three, and it must have been about four when he went away."

If the outrage at Lincolnville had been committed in "the dead of the night," it was perfectly evident to Donald that Captain Shivernock had had nothing whatever to do with it. This conclusion was a great relief to the mind of the young man; but he had hardly reached it before the captain himself passed through the gate, and fixed a searching gaze upon him, as though he regarded him as an interloper.

CHAPTER VII.

LAYING DOWN THE KEEL.

"WHAT are you doing here, Don John?" demanded Captain Shivernock, as he ascended the steps of the piazza.

"I came to see you, sir," replied Donald, respectfully.

"Well, you see me—don't you?"

"I do, sir."

"Have you been talking to Sykes and his wife?" asked the captain, sternly.

"I have, sir."

"Have you told them that you saw me on the island?"

"No, sir; not them, nor anybody else."

"It's well for you that you haven't," added the captain, shaking his head—a significant gesture, which seemed to relate to the future, rather than to the present. "If you lisp a syllable of it, you will need a patch on your skull.—Now,'' he continued, ''what do you want of me?''

''I wanted to talk about the Juno with you. Perhaps I can find a customer for you.''

''Come into the house,'' growled the captain, as he stalked through the door.

Donald followed him into a sitting-room, on one side of which was a secretary, provided with a writing-desk. The captain tossed his cap and overcoat into a chair, and seated himself at the desk. He picked up a quill pen, and began to write as though he intended to scratch a hole through the paper, making noise enough for a small locomotive. He finished the writing, and signed his name to it. Then he cast the contents of a sand-box upon it, returning to it the portion which did not adhere to the paper. The document looked as though it had been written with a handspike, or as though the words had been ploughed in, and a furrow of sand left to form the letters.

''Here!'' said the captain, extending the paper to his visitor, with a jerk, as though he was performing a most ungracious office.

''What is it, sir?'' asked Donald, as he too the document.

"Can't you read?" growled the strange man.

Under ordinary circumstances Donald could read—could read writing when not more than half the letters were merged into straight lines; but it required all his skill, and not a little of his Scotch-Yankee guessing ability, to decipher the vagrant, staggering characters which the captain had impressed with so much force upon the paper. It proved to be a bill of sale of the Juno, in due form, and for the consideration of three hundred dollars.

"Surely you cannot mean this, Captain Shivernock?" exclaimed the amazed young man.

"Can't I? Do you think I'm a lunatic?" stormed the captain.

Donald did think so, but he was not so imprudent as to say it.

"I can't pay you three hundred dollars for the boat," pleaded he.

"Nobody asked you to pay a red cent. The boat is yours. If you don't want her, sell her to the first man who is fool enough to buy her. That's all."

"I'm very grateful to you for your kindness, Captain Shivernock; and I hope—"

"All stuff!" interposed the strange man, savagely. "You are like the rest of the world, and next week you would be as ready to kick me as any other man would be, if you dared to do so. You needn't stop any longer to talk that sort of bosh to me. It will do for Sunday Schools and prayer meetings."

"But I am really—"

"No matter if you are really. Shut up!"

"I hope I shall be able to do something to serve you."

"Bah!"

"Have you heard the news, Captain Shivernock?" asked Donald, suddenly changing the topic.

"What news?"

"It's in the *Age*. A man over in Lincolnville, by the name of Hasbrook, was taken out of his bed last night, and severely beaten."

"Hasbrook! Served him right!" exclaimed the captain, with a rough string of profanity, which cooled the blood of the listener. "He is the biggest scoundrel in the State of Maine, and I am much obliged to the man who did it. I would have taken a hand with him at the game, if I had been there."

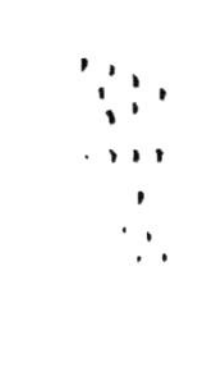

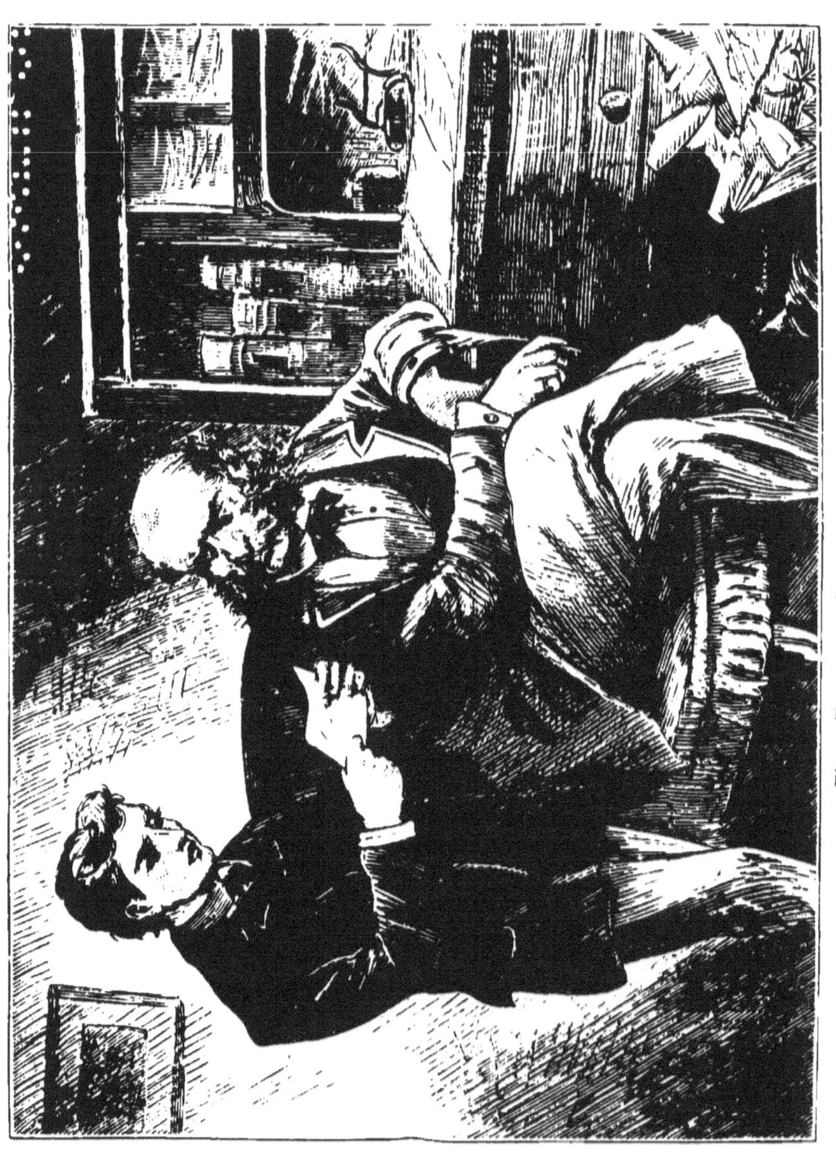

The Bill of Sale. Page 119.

This was equivalent to saying that he was not there.

"Do you know this Hasbrook?" asked Donald.

"Do I know him? He swindled me out of a thousand dollars, and I ought to know him. If the man that flogged him hasn't finished him, I'll pound him myself when I catch him in the right place," replied the strange man, violently. "Who did the job, Don John?"

"I don't know, sir. He hasn't been discovered yet."

"If he is discovered, I'll give him five hundred dollars, and pay the lawyers for keeping him out of jail. I wish I had done it myself; it would make me feel good."

Donald was entirely satisfied that Captain Shivernock had not done it. He was pleased, even rejoiced, that his investigation had resulted so decidedly in the captain's favor, for he would have been very sorry to feel obliged to disregard the injunction of secrecy which had been imposed upon him.

"Did you fall in with any one after we parted this morning?" asked Donald, who desired to know whether the captain had met Laud Cavendish when the two boats appeared to be approaching each other.

"None of your business!" rudely replied the captain, after gazing a moment into the face of the young man, as if to fathom his purpose in asking the question. "Do you think the world won't move on if you don't wind it up? Mind your own business, and don't question me. I won't have anybody prying into my affairs."

"Excuse me, sir; I don't wish to pry into your affairs; and with your permission I will go home now," replied Donald.

"You have my permission to go home," sneered the strange man; and Donald availed himself of it without another instant's delay.

Certainly Captain Shivernock was a very strange man, and Donald could not begin to understand why he had given him the Juno and the sixty dollars in cash. It was plain enough that he had not been near Hasbrook's house, though it was not quite clear how, if he left home at four o'clock, he had got aground eight miles from the city at the same hour; but there was probably some error in Donald's reckoning. The young man went home, and, on the way, having assured himself, to his own satisfaction, that he had no painful duty in regard to the captain to perform, he soon forgot all about the matter in the more engrossing consideration of his great business enterprise. When he entered the cottage, his mother very naturally asked him where he had been; and he gave her all the details of his interview with Mr. Rodman. Mrs. Ramsay was more cheerful than she had been before since the death of her husband, and they discussed the subject till bed time. Donald had seventy-two dollars in his pocket, including his fees for measuring the yachts. It was a new experience for him to keep anything from his mother; but he felt that he could not honorably tell her what had passed between the captain and himself. He could soon work the money into his business, and he need keep it only till Monday. He did not feel just right about it, even after he had convinced himself that he ought not to reveal Captain Shivernock's secret to her; but I must add, confidentially, that it is always best for boys—I mean young men—to tell their mothers "all about it;" and if Donald had done so in this instance, no harm would have come of the telling, and it might have saved him a great deal of trouble, and her a great deal of anxiety, and a great many painful doubts. Donald thought his view was correct; he meant to do exactly right; and he had the courage to do it, even if thereby he incurred the wrath and the vengeance of the strange man.

I have no doubt, from what indications I have of the character of Donald Ramsay, that he tried to learn his Sunday School lesson, tried to give attention to the sermons he heard, and tried to be interested in the good books he essayed to read on Sunday; but I am not sure that he succeeded entirely, for the skeleton frame of the Maud would rise up in his imagination to cloud the vision of higher things, and the remembrance of his relations with Captain Shivernock would thrust itself upon him. Yet it is a great deal even to try to be faithful in one's thoughts, and Donald was generally more successful than on this occasion, for it was not often that he was excited by events so stirring and prospects so brilliant. A single week would be time enough to accustom the young boat-builder to his occupation and restore his mental equilibrium.

The light of Monday morning's sun was very welcome to him; and when only its light gleamed in the gray east, he rose from his bed to begin the labors of the day. His father had enlarged the shop, so that he could build a yacht of the size of the Maud under its roof; and before breakfast time, he had prepared the bed, and levelled the blocks on which the keel was to rest. At seven o'clock Lawrence Kennedy appeared, and together they looked over the stock on hand, and made out a list of the pieces of timber and plank that would be required. At first the journeyman was inclined to take the lead in the business; but he soon found that his youthful employer was entirely familiar with the minutest details of the work, and knew precisely how to get out every stick of the frame. Donald constantly referred to the model of the Sea Foam, which he had already altered in accordance with the suggestions of his father, using the inch scale on which the model was projected, to get the size of the pieces, so that there should be no unnecessary waste in buying.

Kennedy went with him to the lumber wharf, where the stock was carefully selected for the frame. Before dinner it was carted over to the shop, and in the afternoon the work was actually commenced. The keelson, with the aperture for the centre-board nicely adjusted, was laid down, levelled, and blocked up, so that the yacht should be as true as a hair when completed. The next steps were to set up the stern-post and the stem-piece, and Mr. Ramsay's patterns of these timbers were ready for use. Donald was tired enough to rest when the clock struck six; but no better day's work for two men could be shown than that performed by him and his journeyman. Another hand could now work to advantage on the frame, and Kennedy knew of a first-rate workman who desired employment. He was requested to have him in the shop the next morning.

After supper, Donald went back to the shop to study, rather than to work. He seated himself on the bench, and was thinking over the details of the work, when, through the window, he saw Laud Cavendish run his sail-boat alongside the Juno, which was moored a short distance from the shore. Laud wanted to buy a boat, and Donald wanted to sell one. More than once he had been tempted to keep the Juno for his own use; but he decided that he could not afford such a luxury, even though she had cost him nothing. If he kept her, he would desire to use her, and he might waste too much of his precious time in sailing her. It would cost money as well as time to keep her; for boats are always in need of paint, spars, sails, rigging, and other repairs. He was resolute in his purpose to dispose of the Juno, lest the possession of her should demoralize him, and interfere with his attention to business.

It was plain enough to Donald that he must sell the Juno, though it was not as clear that Laud Cavendish could buy her; but he decided to see him, and, launching his tender, he pulled out for the Juno. While he was plying his oars, it suddenly came across the mind of the young boat-builder that he could not sell this boat without exposing his relations to Captain Shivernock. He was rather startled by the thought, but, before he had followed it out to a conclusion, the tender was alongside the Juno.

"How are you, Don John?" said Laud. "I thought I would come down and look over the Juno."

"She is a first-rate boat," replied Donald.

"And the captain wants to sell her?"

"She's for sale," replied her owner.

"What's the price of her?"

"Four hundred."

"That's too steep, Don John. It is of no use for me to look at her if the captain won't sell her for less than that."

"Say three fifty, then," replied Donald.

"Say three hundred."

"She is worth more money," continued the owner, as he unlocked the cuddy. "She has a fine cabin, fitted up like a parlor. Go in and look round."

Donald led the way, and pointed out all the conveniences of the cabin, eloquently setting forth the qualities of the boat and her accommodations.

"I'll give three hundred for her," said Laud.

"She is worth more than that," replied Donald. "Why, she cost the captain over five hundred; and I wouldn't build her for a mill less than that."

"You?" laughed Laud.

"I'm building a yacht thirty feet long for Sam Rodman; and I'm to have twelve hundred for her," answered Donald, struggling to be modest.

“You are some punkins—arn’t you, Don John?”

“I can’t quite come up to you, Mr. Cavendish.”

“Perhaps you will when you are as old as I am.”

“Possibly; but it’s a big height to reach in two years. A man of your size ought not to haggle for fifty dollars on a boat.”

“I can’t afford to give more than three hundred for the Juno,” protested Laud, very decidedly.

“Can you afford to give that?” asked Donald, with a smile.

Laud looked at him sharply, and seemed to be somewhat embarrassed.

“I suppose I can’t really afford it; but what’s life for? We can’t live it over again, and we ought to make the best of it. Don’t you think so?”

“Certainly—the best of it; but there may be some difference of opinion in regard to what the best of it may be.”

“I mean to be a gentleman, and not a philosopher. I go in for a good time. Will you take three hundred for the boat? or will you tell the captain I will give that?”

9

"I can sell her without going to him. I haven't offered her to anybody but you, and I have no doubt I can get my price for her."

Laud talked till it was nearly dark; but Donald was firm, and at last he carried his point.

"I will give the three hundred and fifty, because I want her very badly; but it's a big price," said Laud.

"It's dog cheap," added Donald, who was beginning to think how he should manage the business without informing the purchaser that the Juno was his own property.

Donald was a young man of many expedients, and he finally decided to ask Captain Shivernock to exchange the bill of sale for one conveying the boat directly to Laud Cavendish. This settled, he wondered how Laud expected to pay for his purchase, for it was utterly incredible to him that the swell could command so large a sum as three hundred and fifty dollars. After all, perhaps it would not be necessary to trouble the captain about the business, for Donald did not intend to give a bill of sale without the cash.

"When do you want to close the trade?" he asked.

"I thought we had closed it," replied Laud.

"You want a bill of sale—don't you?"

"No, I don't; I would rather not have one. When I get the boat, I know how to keep her. Besides, you will be a witness that I have bought her."

"That isn't the way to do business," protested Donald.

"If I'm satisfied, you need not complain. If I pay you the cash down,that ends the matter."

"If you do."

"Well, I will; here and now," added Laud, pulling out his wallet.

"Where did you get so much money, Laud?" asked Donald.

It was doubtless an impertinent question, but it came from the heart of him who proposed it; and it was not resented by him to whom it was put. On the contrary, Laud seemed to be troubled, rather than indignant.

"Don John, you are a good fellow," said Laud, after a long pause.

"Of course I am."

"For certain reasons of my own, I want you to keep this trade to yourself."

"Why so?"

"I can't tell you."

"Then I won't do it. If there is any hitch about the money, I won't have anything to do with it."

"Any hitch? What do you mean by that?" demanded Laud, with a lofty air.

"It's no use to mince the matter, Laud. Three hundred and fifty dollars don't grow on every bush in your or my garden; and I have been wondering, all the time, where a fellow like you should get money enough to buy a boat like the Juno."

Donald said all this fairly and squarely; but it occurred to him just then, that after he had sold the boat, any one might ask him the same question, and he should not feel at liberty to answer it.

"Do you mean to insult me?" demanded Laud.

"Nothing of the sort; and you needn't ride that high horse. I won't sell the boat till I know where the money came from."

"Do you doubt my honor?"

"Confound your honor! I think we have said enough."

"If you mean to say that I didn't come honorably by my money, you are mistaken."

"Where did you get it, then?"

"Are you always willing to tell where you get every dollar in your pocket?" retorted Laud.

That was a home-thrust, and Donald felt it in his trowsers pocket, where he kept his wallet.

"I am generally ready to tell where I get my money," he replied, but he did not speak with much energy.

Laud looked about him, and seemed to be considering the matter.

"I don't like to be accused of stealing," mused he.

"I don't accuse you of anything," added Donald.

"It's the same thing. If I tell you where I got this money, will you keep it to yourself?" asked Laud.

"If it's all right I will."

"Honor bright, Don John?"

"If it's all right."

"O, it is!" protested Laud. "I will tell you; but you must keep the secret, whatever happens."

"I will, if everything is as it should be."

"Well, Captain Shivernock gave it to me," said Laud, in confidential tones, and after looking about to satisfy himself that no third person was within hearing.

"Captain Shivernock!" exclaimed Donald.

"Just so."

"What for?"

"I can't tell you any more. The captain would kill me if he found out that I had told you so much," answered Laud. "I don't understand the matter myself; but the captain gave me that money and fifty dollars more;" and he handed Donald the price of the Juno. "You are not to say that I have even seen the captain."

"When was this?"

"Last Saturday; but that's all; not another word from me."

"It's very odd," mused Donald.

"You will keep still—won't you?"

"Yes; until I am satisfied the thing is not all right."

"I shall not say that I own the Juno yet a while," added Laud, as he returned to the boat in which he had come.

Donald pulled ashore, with the money in his pocket.

CHAPTER VIII.

THE FIRST REGATTA.

DONALD was not disposed to doubt the truth of Laud Cavendish's story, for the circumstances were precisely the same as those under which he had received the boat and the money from Captain Shivernock. If he had had no experience with the eccentric shipmaster himself, he would have doubted the whole explanation, and refused to take the money. He recalled the events of Saturday. The last he saw of Laud, on that day, was when he ran his boat over towards the Northport shore, whither the captain had gone before him. He had lost sight of both their boats at a time when it seemed very probable that they would meet. After what Laud had just said to him, and with the money he had paid him in his pocket, he was confident they had met. The strange man had purchased the silence of

Laud, as he had his own, and at about the same price.

Donald realized that Captain Shivernock had thrown away about seven hundred dollars that morning, and, as he thought of it, he was amazed at his conduct; but the captain did not mind paying a thousand dollars any time to gratify the merest whim. The young man tried again to fathom the motive of his eccentric but liberal patron in thus throwing away such large sums, unnecessarily large, to accomplish his object. The Lincolnville outrage was the only possible solution; but if he were the ruffian, he would not have been on Long Island when he had a fair wind to run home, and Sykes and his wife both agreed that he had left the house on the morning that Donald had seen him. It was not possible, therefore, that the captain was guilty of the outrage. Laud had paid him seven fifty dollar bills, and he had over four hundred dollars in his pocket. He did not know what to do with it, and feeling that he had come honestly by it, he was vexed at the necessity of concealing it from his mother; but he was determined to pay it out, as occasion required, for stock and hardware for the yacht he was building. When he went to his chamber, he concealed three hundred and fifty dollars of the money in a secret place in the pine bureau in which his clothes were kept.

The next morning Kennedy appeared with the man he was authorized to employ, and the chips flew briskly in the shop all that day. At noon Donald went to the wharf where he had bought his stock, and paid the bill for it. The lumber dealer commended his promptness, and offered to give him credit for any lumber he might need; but Donald proudly declared that he should pay cash for all he bought, and he wanted the lowest cash prices. On his return to the shop, he entered, in the account-book his father had kept, the amount he had expended. The work went bravely on, for his two journeymen were interested in his success. They were glad to get employment, and desired that the young boat-builder should not only build a fine yacht, but should make money by the job. The stem-piece and stern-post were set up, and gradually the frame began to assume the shape of a vessel. Donald watched the forming of the yacht very carefully, and saw that everything was done according to the model and the scale.

On Saturday morning Mr. Rodman, accompanied by a friend who was a ship-builder, visited the shop to inspect the work. The frame, so far as it had been set up, was carefully examined, and the expert cordially approved all that had been done, declaring that he had never seen a better job in his life. Of course Donald was proud of this partial success.

"I have had some doubts, Don John," laughed Mr. Rodman; "but I am entirely satisfied now."

"Thank you, sir. I have had no doubts; I could see that frame in my mind as plainly before a stick had been touched as I do now."

"You have done well, and I am quite sure that you will make a yacht of it. Now, if you will give me a receipt for one hundred dollars, I will let you have so much towards the price of the Maud, for I suppose you want to pay your men off to-night."

"I have money enough, sir, to pay my men, and I don't ask you for any money yet," replied the young boat-builder.

"But I prefer to pay you as the work progresses."

Donald did not object, and wrote the receipt.

He was a minor, and his mother, who was the administratrix of her husband's estate, was the responsible party in the transaction of business; but he did not like to sign his mother's name to a receipt, and thus wholly ignore himself, and, adopting a common fiction in trade, he wrote, "Ramsay and son," which he determined should be the style of the firm. "Ramsay might mean his father or his mother, and he had already arranged this matter with her. Mr. Rodman laughed at the signature, but did not object to it, and Donald put the money in his pocket, after crediting it on the book.

This was the day appointed for the first regatta of the Yacht Club. The coming event had been talked about in the city during the whole week, not only among the boys, but among the men who were interested in yachting. About a dozen yachts had been entered for the race, though only four of them belonged to the club; those that were not enrolled being nominally in charge of members, in order to conform to the regulations. Donald had measured all these boats, and made a schedule of them, in which appeared the captain's name, the length of the craft, with the correction to be subtracted from the sailing time in order to reduce it to standard time. There were columns in the table for the starting time, the return time, and the sailing time. The "correction" was virtually the allowance which a large yacht made to a smaller one for the difference in length.

The club had adopted the regulation of the Dorchester Yacht Club, which contained a "table of allowance per mile." In this table, a yacht one hundred and ten feet six inches long, is taken as the standard for length. The Skylark was just thirty feet long on the water-line, and her allowance by the table was two minutes forty-three and four tenths seconds for every mile sailed in a regatta. The Sea Foam's length was three inches less, and her allowance was one and three tenths seconds more. Donald had his table all ready for the use of the judges, of whom he had been appointed the chairman. Mr. Montague's large yacht had been anchored in the bay, gayly dressed with flags and streamers, to be used as the judges' boat. The yachts were to start at ten o'clock.

"I don't want to leave my work a bit," said Donald, as he took off his apron. "I may have to lose a whole day in the race, and I can't afford it."

"Now, I think you can," replied Kennedy.

"It looks too much like boys' play."

"No matter what it is. If you are going to make a business of building yachts and sail-boats, it is for your interest to encourage this sort of thing all you can," added Kennedy.

"I think you are right there," answered Donald, who had not before taken this view.

"Besides, you ought to see how the boats work. You will get some ideas that will be of use to you. You should observe every movement of the boats with the utmost care. I think you will make more money attending the regattas, if there was one every week, than by working in the shop."

"You are right, Kennedy, and I am glad you expressed your opinions, for I shall feel that I am not wasting my time."

"Your father has been to Newport and New York on purpose to attend regattas, and I am sure, if he were here now, he would not miss this race for a fifty-dollar bill," continued the workman.

Donald was entirely satisfied, and went into the house to dress for the occasion. He was soon

ready, and walked down the beach towards the
skiff he used to go off to the sail-boat. The sky
was overcast, and the wind blew a smashing
breeze, promising a lively race. The Juno had
been entered for the regatta, but she was still at
her moorings off the shop, and Donald wondered
where Laud was, for he had been very enthusiastic over the event. Before he could embark, the
new proprietor of the Juno appeared. He was
dressed in a suit of new clothes, wore a new
round-top hat, and sported a cane in his hand.
His mustache had been freshly colored, and every
hair was carefully placed. He did not look like
a yachtman; more like a first-class swell.

"I have been all the morning looking for some
fellows to sail with me," said Laud. "I can't
find a single one. Won't you go with me, Don
John?"

"Thank you; I am one of the judges, and I
can't go," replied Donald, who, if he had not
been engaged, would have preferred to sail with
some more skilful and agreeable skipper than
Laud Cavendish.

"Won't your men go with me?"

"I don't know; you can ask them."

"I am entitled to carry five, and I want some live weights to-day, for it is blowing fresh," added Laud, as he walked towards the shop.

Neither of Donald's men was willing to lose his time, and as Laud came out of the shop, he discovered a young lady walking up the beach towards the city. A gust of wind blew her hat away at this moment, and Mr. Cavendish gallantly ran after, and recovered it, as Donald would have done if he had not been anticipated, for he recognized the young lady as soon as he saw her. Even as it was, he was disposed to run after that hat, and dispute the possession of it with Mr. Laud Cavendish, for the owner thereof was Miss Nellie Patterdale.

"Allow me to return your truant hat, Miss Patterdale," said Laud.

"Thank you, Mr. Cavendish," replied Nellie, rather coldly, as she resumed her walk towards the place where Donald stood, a few rods farther up the beach.

"We have a fine breeze for the race, Miss Patterdale," added Laud, smirking and jerking, as though he intended to improve the glorious opportunity, for the young lady was not only bewitchingly pretty, but her father was a nabob, with only two children.

"Very fine, I should think," she answered; and her tones and manner were anything but encouraging to the aspirant.

"I hope you are going to honor the gallant yachtmen with your presence, Miss Patterdale."

"I shall certainly see the race.—Good morning, Don John," said she, when she came within speaking distance of Donald.

"Good morning, Nellie," replied he, blushing, as he felt the full force of her glance and her smile—a glance and a smile for which Laud would have sacrificed all he held dear in the world, even to his cherished mustache. "Don't you attend the race?"

"Yes, I want to attend now. Ned invited me to go on board of the judge's boat; but the sun was out then, and mother would not let me go. Father said the day would be cloudy, and I decided to go; but Ned had gone. I came down here to see if I couldn't hail him. Won't you take me off to the Penobscot in your boat?"

"Certainly I will, with the greatest pleasure," replied Donald, with enthusiasm.

"I beg your pardon, Miss Patterdale," interposed Laud. "I am going off in the Juno; allow me to tender her for your use. I can take you off, Don John, at the same time."

"It's quite rough, as you see, Nellie, and the Juno is much larger than my boat. You can go in her more comfortably than in mine," added Donald.

"Thank you; just as you please, Don John," she answered.

"Bring her up to the wharf, Mr. Cavendish," continued Donald.

Laud leaped into his skiff, and pulled off to the Juno, while Nellie and Donald walked around to the wharf. In a few moments the boat was ready, and came up to the pier, though her clumsy skipper was so excited at the prospect of having the nabob's pretty daughter in his boat, that he had nearly smashed her against the timbers. The gallant skipper bowed, and smirked, and smiled, as he assisted Miss Patterdale to a place in the standing-room. Donald shoved off the bow, and the Juno filled her mainsail, and went off flying towards the Penobscot.

10

"It's a smashing breeze," said Donald, as the boat heeled down.

"Glorious!" exclaimed Laud. "Are you fond of sailing, Miss Patterdale?"

"I am very fond of it."

"Perhaps you would like to sail around the course in one of the yachts?" suggested the skipper.

"I should be delighted to do so," she replied, eagerly; and she glanced at Donald, as if to ascertain if such a thing were possible.

"I should be pleased to have you sail in the Juno," added Laud, with an extra smirk.

"Thank you, Mr. Cavendish; you are very kind; but perhaps I had better not go."

"I should be delighted to have you go with me."

"I don't think you would enjoy it, Nellie," said Donald. "It blows fresh, and the Juno is rather wet in a heavy sea."

Laud looked at him with an angry expression, and when Nellie turned away from him, he made significant gestures to induce Donald to unsay what he had said, and persuade her to go with him.

"I am sure you will be delighted with the sail, Miss Patterdale. You will be perfectly dry where you are sitting; or, if not, I have a rubber coat, which will protect you."

"I think I will not go," she replied, so coldly that her tones would have frozen any one but a simpleton like Laud.

The passage was of brief duration, and Donald assisted Nellie up the accommodation steps of the Penobscot, stepping forward in season to deprive Laud of this pleasant office.

"I am much obliged to you, Mr. Cavendish," said she, walking away from the steps.

. "That was mean of you, Don John," muttered Laud, as Donald came down the steps to assist in shoving off the Juno.

"What was mean?"

"Why, to tell Nellie she would not enjoy the sail with me."

"She could do as she pleased."

"But you told her the Juno was wet," added Laud, angrily.

"She is wet when it blows."

"No matter if she is. It was mean of you to say anything about it, after all I have done for you."

"It wasn't mean to tell the truth, and save her from a ducking, and I don't know what you have done for me."

"You don't? Didn't I buy this boat of you, and pay you fifty dollars more than she is worth?"

"No, you didn't. But if you are dissatisfied with your bargain, I will take her off your hands."

"You! I want the money I paid."

"You shall have it. Come to the shop after the race, and you may throw up the trade."

"Will Captain Shivernock pay you back the money?" sneered Laud.

"I'll take care of that, if you want to give her up," added Donald, warmly.

"Never mind that now. Can't you persuade Nellie to sail with me?" continued Laud, more gently. "If you will, I will give you a five-dollar bill."

Donald would have given double that sum rather than have had her go with him, and she would have given ten times the amount to avoid doing so.

"I can't persuade her, for I don't think it is best for her to go," replied Donald.

"No matter what you think. You are a good fellow, Don John: do this for me—won't you? It would be a great favor, and I shall never forget it."

"Why do you want her to go with you?" demanded Donald, rather petulantly. "A yacht in a race is no place for ladies. I can find some fellows on board here who will be glad to go with you."

"But I want her to go with me. The fact of it is, Don John, I rather like Nellie, and I want to be better acquainted with her."

"If you do, you must paddle your own canoe," replied Donald, indignantly, as he ascended the steps, and joined the other two judges on deck.

"We are waiting for you, Don John," said Sam Rodman, who was one of them.

"It isn't ten yet, and I have the papers all ready. Who is to be time-keeper?" asked the chairman.

"I have a watch with a second hand, and I will take that office," said Frank Norwood, who was the third.

Most of the yachts were already in line, and the captain of the fleet, in the tender of his yacht, was arranging them, the largest to windward. The first gun had been fired at half past nine, which was the signal to get into line, and at the next, the yachts were to get under way. All sail except the jib was set, and at the signal each craft was to slip her cable, hoist her jib, if she had one, and get under way, as quickly as possible. The "rode" was simply to be cast off, for the end of it was made fast to the tender, which was used as a buoy for the anchor.

"Are they all ready?" asked Donald, as the time drew near.

"All but the Juno. Laud has picked up two live weights, and wants another man," replied Sam Rodman.

"We won't wait for him."

But Laud got into line in season. One of the seamen of the Penobscot stood at the lock-string of the gun forward, ready to fire when the chairman of the judges gave the word.

"Have your watch ready, Frank," said Donald.

"All ready," answered Norwood.

"Fire!" shouted Donald.

Some of the ladies "squealed" when the gun went off, but all eyes were immediately directed to the yachts. The Christabel, with a reef in her fore and main sails, was next to the Penobscot; then came the Skylark, the Sea Foam, and the Phantom. Before the gun was fired, the captain had stationed a hand in each yacht at the cable, and others at the jib-halyards and downhauls. The instant the gun was discharged, the jibs were run up, and the "rodes" thrown overboard. Some of the yachts, however, were unfortunate, and did not obtain a good start. In one the jib down-haul fouled, and another ran over her cable, and swamped her tender. The conflict was believed to be between the Skylark and the Sea Foam, for there was too much wind for the Christabel, which was the fastest lightweather craft in the line.

It was a beautiful sight when the yachts went off, with the wind only a little abaft the beam. The young gentlemen sailing them were rather excited, and made some mistakes. The Skylark at once took the lead, for Commodore Montague was the most experienced boatman in the fleet. He made no mistakes, and his superior skill was soon evident in the distance between him and the Sea Foam.

The crowd of people on the shore and the judges' yacht watched the contestants till they disappeared beyond Turtle Head. The boats had a free wind both ways, with the exception of a short distance beyond the head, where they had to beat up to Stubb's Point Ledge. There was nothing for the judges to do until the yachts came in, and Donald spent a couple of delightful hours with Nellie Patterdale. Presently the Skylark appeared again beyond the Head, leading the fleet as before. On she drove, like a bolt from an arrow, carrying a big bone in her mouth; and the judges prepared to take her time.

CHAPTER IX.

THE SKYLARK AND THE SEA FOAM.

FRANK NORWOOD was the time-keeper, and he stood with his watch in his hand. Each yacht was to pass to windward of the Penobscot, and come round her stern, reporting as she did so. Sam Rodman was to call "time" when the foremast of each yacht was in range with a certain chimney of a house on the main shore. At the word Frank was to give the time, and Donald was to write it down on his schedule. Everything was to be done with the utmost accuracy. The Skylark was rapidly approaching, with the Sea Foam nearly half a mile astern of her. The Phantom and Christabel were not far behind the Sea Foam, while the rest were scattered along all the way over to Turtle Head.

"Ready there!" shouted Donald, as the Skylark came nearly in range of the Penobscot and the chimney.

"All ready," replied Sam Rodman.

The gun forward had been loaded, and a seaman stood at the lock-string, to salute the first boat in.

"Time!" shouted Sam, as the mainsail of the Skylark shut in the chimney on the shore; and the six-pounder awoke the echoes among the hills.

"Twelve, forty, and thirty-two seconds," added Frank, as he took the time from the watch.

"Twelve, forty, thirty-two," repeated Donald, as he wrote it on the schedule.

The crowd on the judges' yacht cheered the commodore as the Skylark rounded the Penobscot, and the ladies waved their handkerchiefs at him with desperate enthusiasm.

"I thought you said the Sea Foam was to beat the Skylark," said Nellie Patterdale.

"I think she may do it yet," replied Donald.

"And Sam's new boat must beat them both, Don John," laughed Maud Rodman.

"Time!" called Sam.

"Twelve, forty-five, two," added Frank.

"Twelve, forty-five, two," repeated Donald, writing down the time.

By this time the Skylark had come about, not

by gybing,—for the wind was too heavy to make this evolution in safety,—but had come round head to the wind, and now passed under the stern of the Penobscot.

"Skylark!" reported the commodore.

A few minutes later the Sea Foam did the same. The Phantom came in a minute after the Sea Foam, and for a few moments the judges were very busy taking the time of the next four boats. The Juno did not arrive till half past one, and she was the last one. As fast as the yachts rounded the Penobscot, they went off to the line and picked up their cables and anchors. The captains of the several craft which had sailed in the race then boarded the Penobscot to ascertain the decision of the judges.

"You waxed me badly, Robert," said Ned Patterdale, who was mortified at the defeat of the Sea Foam, though he kept good-natured about it.

"I still think the Skylark can't be beaten by anything of her inches," replied Commodore Montague.

"I am rather disappointed in the Sea Foam," added Ned.

Donald heard this remark, and he was much

disturbed by it; for it seemed like a reproach upon the skill of his father, and an imputation upon the reputation of Ramsay and Son. If the yachts built by the "firm" were beaten as badly as the Sea Foam had been, though she had out-sailed the Phantom, it would seriously injure the business of the concern. The defeat of the Sea Foam touched the boat-builder in a tender place, and he found it necessary to do something to maintain the standing of the firm. He knew just what the matter was; but under ordinary circum-stances he would not have said a word to damage the pride of the present owner of the Sea Foam.

"I am sorry you are not satisfied with her, Ned," said Donald.

"But I expected too much of her; for I thought she was going to beat the Skylark," replied Ned Patterdale. "I think you encouraged me some-what in that direction, Don John."

"I did; and I still think she can beat the Sky-lark."

"It's no use to think so; for she has just beaten me four minutes and a half; and that's half a mile in this breeze. Nothing could have been more fairly done."

"It was all perfectly fair, Ned; but you know that winning a race does not depend entirely upon the boat," suggested Donald, hinting mildly at his own theory of the defeat.

"Then you think I didn't sail her well?" said Ned.

"I think you sailed her very well; but it could not be expected that you would do as well with her as Bob Montague with the Skylark, for he has sailed his yacht for months, while you have only had yours a few weeks. This is a matter of business with me, Ned. If our boats are beaten, we lose our work. It is bread and butter to me."

"If it was my fault, I am sorry she was beaten, for your sake, Don John; but I did my best with her," replied Ned, with real sympathy for his friend.

"Of course I am not going to cry over spilt milk."

"Do you really think the Sea Foam can beat the Skylark?"

"I think so; but I may be mistaken. At any rate, I should like the chance to sail the Sea Foam with the Skylark. I don't consider it exactly an even thing between you and the commodore, because he has had so much more experience than you have," replied Donald.

"You believe you can sail the Sea Foam better than I can—do you, Don John?"

"It wouldn't be pleasant for me to say that, Ned."

"But that's what you mean?"

"I have explained the reason why I spoke of this matter at all, Ned. It is bread and butter to me, and I hope you don't think I am vain."

Ned was a little vexed at the remarks of his friend, and rather indignant at his assumed superiority as a boatman. Donald was usually very modest and unpretentious. He was not in the habit of claiming that he could do anything better than another. Generally, in boating matters, when he saw that a thing was done wrong, he refrained from criticising unless his opinion was asked, and was far from being forward in fault-finding. Though he was an authority among the young men in sailing boats, he had not attained this distinction by being a critic and caviller. Ned was therefore surprised, as well as indignant, at the comments and the assumption of Donald; but a little reflection enabled him to see the boat-builder's motive, which was anything but vanity. He had some of this weakness himself, and felt that he had sailed the Sea Foam as well as any one could have done it, and was satisfied that the Skylark was really a faster yacht than his own. The race was plain sailing, with a free wind nearly all the way, and there was not much room for the exercise of superior skill in handling the craft. At least, this was Ned's opinion. If the course had been a dead beat to windward for ten miles, the case would have been different; and Ned had failed to notice that he had lost half the distance between the Skylark and the Sea Foam when he rounded the stake buoy.

It was a fact that among the large party on board the Penobscot, the boats of the firm of Ramsay and Son were just then at a discount, and those of the Newport builders at a corresponding premium. Donald was grieved and vexed, and trembled for the future of the firm of which he was the active representative. But he figured up the results of the race, and when the captains of all the yachts had come on board of the judges' boat, he announced the prizes and delivered them to the winners, with a little speech. The silver vase was given to the commodore, with liberal and magnanimous commendations both of the yacht and her captain. The marine glass was presented to Edward Patterdale, as the winner of the second prize, with some pleasant words, which did not in the least betray the personal discomfiture of the chairman. There was a further ceremony on the quarter-deck of the Penobscot, which was not in the programme, and which was unexpected to all except the officers of the club.

"Captain Laud Cavendish, of the Juno," said the chairman of the judges, who stood on the trunk of the yacht, where all on board, as well as those in the boats collected around her, could see him.

Laud stepped forward, wondering what the call could mean.

"I find, after figuring up the results of the race," continued the chairman, glancing at the schedule he held in his hand, "that you are entitled to the third and last prize. By carefully timing the movements of your excellent craft, and by your superior skill in sailing her, you have contrived to come in—last in the race; and the officers of the club have instructed the judges to award this medal to you. I have the honor and the very great pleasure of suspending it around your neck.''

The medal was made of sole leather, about six inches in diameter. Attached to it was a yard of stove-pipe chain, by which it was hung around the neck of the winner of the *last* prize. A shout of laughter and a round of applause greeted the presentation of the medal. Laud did not know whether to smile or get mad; for he felt like the victim of a practical joke. Miss Nellie Patterdale stood near him, and perhaps her presence restrained an outburst of anger. Mr. Montague, the father of the commodore, had provided a bountiful collation in the cabin of the Penobscot, and the next half hour was given up to the discussion of the repast. Laud tried to make himself agreeable to Nellie, and the poor girl was persecuted by his attentions until she was obliged to break away from him.

''Don John, I am told that everybody is satisfied with this race except you,'' said Commodore Montague, as the party went on deck after the collation.

11

"I am satisfied with it," replied Donald. "Everything has been perfectly fair, and the Sky·lark has beaten the Sea Foam."

"But you still think the Sea Foam can outsail the Skylark?"

"I think so; but of course I may be mistaken."

"You believe that Ned Patterdale didn't get all her speed out of the Sea Foam," added the commodore.

"I don't mean to say a word to disparage Ned; but he don't know the Sea Foam as you do the Skylark."

"There is hardly a particle of difference between the boats."

"I know it; but you have had so much more experience than Ned, that he ought not to be expected to compete with you. If you will exchange boats, and you do your best in the Sea Foam, I believe you would beat your own yacht. I think Ned does first rate for the experience he has had."

"So do I; but I believe the difference is in the sailing of the boats; for you may build two yachts as near alike as possible, and one of them will do better than the other," said Robert Montague.

"I should like to have you sail the Sea Foam against the Skylark, Bob," added Donald.

"You don't want me to beat my own boat, if I can—do you, Don John?" laughed Robert.

"I think you could."

"I'll tell you what I'll do: I'll sail the Skylark against the Sea Foam this afternoon, and you shall handle Ned's yacht. I have been talking with him about it, and he agrees to it."

"I'm willing, Bob," replied Donald, eagerly.

"All right."

"I hope Ned don't think hard of me for speaking of this matter," added Donald. "I wouldn't have uttered a word if this result did not affect our business."

"I understand it, Don John; and so does Ned. But I think you are making a mistake; for if the Sea Foam is beaten again by the Skylark,—as I believe she will be,—it will be all the worse for your firm," laughed Robert.

"I am willing to run the risk," replied Donald. "If we can't build a boat as fast as the Skylark, I want to know it."

"But, Don John, you don't expect me to *let* you beat me—do you?"

"Certainly not, Bob. I hope you will do your very best, and I shall be satisfied with the result."

It was soon reported over the Penobscot that another race was to be sailed immediately, and the report created intense excitement when the circumstances of the affair were explained. Judges were appointed, and other arrangements concluded. Donald and Ned Patterdale went on board of the Sea Foam, and Commodore Montague on board of the Skylark. The two yachts anchored in line, with the Skylark to windward, as she was three inches longer than the other. The start was to be made at the firing of the first gun. Donald took his place at the helm of the Sea Foam, and stationed the hands. He was a little afraid that Ned Patterdale was not as enthusiastic as he might be; for if his yacht won the race, the responsibility for the loss of the first prize in the regatta would rest upon him, and not upon his craft. It would not be so pleasant for him to know that he had failed, in any degree, as a skipper. The position of Donald, therefore, was not wholly agreeable; for he did not like to prove that his friend was deficient in skill, though the future prosperity of the firm of Ramsay and Son required him to do so.

The wind was even fresher than before, and dark clouds indicated a heavy rain before night; but Donald did not heed the weather. He stationed Ned in the standing-room to tend the jib-sheets and mind the centre-board. Two hands were at the cable, and two more at the jib-halyards.

"Are you all ready forward?" called the skipper *pro tem.* of the Sea Foam.

"All ready," replied the hands. And Donald waited with intense interest for the gun.

Bang.

"Let go! Hoist the jib!" cried Donald.

The hands forward worked with a will. The rope was thrown into the tender, to which the end of it was made fast, and the jib, crackling and banging in the stiff breeze, now almost a gale, went up in an instant.

"Haul down the lee jib-sheet," said Donald to his companion in the standing-room. And it is but fair to say that Ned worked as briskly as the yachtmen at the bow.

The Sea Foam heeled over, as the blast struck her sails, till her rail went under; but Donald knew just what she would bear, and kept the tiller stiff in his hand. Stationing Dick Adams at the main sheet behind him, he placed the others upon the weather side. In a moment more the yacht came to her bearings, and lying well over, she flew off on her course. She had made a capital start, and the Skylark was equally fortunate in this respect. The two yachts went off abeam of each other, and for half a mile neither gained a hair upon the other. Then commenced the struggle for the victory. First the Skylark gained a few inches; then the Sea Foam made half a length, though she immediately lost it; for in these relative positions, she came under the lee of her opponent.

Again the Skylark forged ahead, and was a length in advance of the Sea Foam, when the yachts came up with Turtle Head.

"You are losing it, Don John," said Ned, apparently not much displeased at the result.

"Not yet," replied Donald. "A pull on the main sheet, Dick," added the skipper, as he put the helm down. "Give her six inches more centre-board, Ned."

"You will be on the rocks, Don John!" shouted the owner of the yacht, as the Sea Foam dashed under the stern of the Skylark, and ran in close to the shore.

"Don't be alarmed, Ned. Haul down the jib-sheet a little more! Steady! Belay!" said the confident skipper.

By this manœuvre the Sea Foam gained a position to windward of her rival; but she ran within half her breadth of beam of the dangerous rocks, and Ned expected every instant the race would end in a catastrophe. She went clear, however; for Donald knew just the depth of water at any time of tide. Both yachts were now under the lee of the island, and went along more gently than before. It was plain enough now that the Sea Foam had the advantage. Beyond the Head, and near the ledge, she was obliged to brace up to the wind, in order to leave the buoy on the port, as required by the rule. Donald kept her moving very lively, and when she had made her two tacks, she had weathered the buoy, and, rounding it, she gybed so near the ledge that the commodore could not have crawled in between him and the buoy if he had been near enough to do so. Hauling up the centre-board, and letting off the sheets, the Sea Foam went for a time before the wind.

When the Skylark had rounded the buoy, and laid her course for Turtle Head again, she was at least an eighth of a mile astern of her rival. Donald hardly looked at her, but gazed steadfastly at the sails and the shore of the island. The sheets had to be hauled in little by little, as she followed the contour of the land, till at the point below Turtle Head the yacht had the wind forward of the beam. Then came the home stretch, and the skipper trimmed his sails, adjusted the centre-board, and stationed his crew as live weights with the utmost care. It was only necessary for him to hold his own in order to win the race, and he was painfully anxious for the result.

In the Skylark the commodore saw just where he had lost his advantage, and regretted too late that he had permitted the Sea Foam to get to windward of him; but he strained every nerve to recover his position. The wind continued to freshen, and probably both yachts would have done better with a single reef in the mainsail; but there was no time to reduce sail. As they passed Turtle Head and came out into the open bay, the white-capped waves broke over the bows,

Donald sailing the Sea Foam.   Page 166.

dashing the spray from stem to stern. Neither Donald nor Robert flinched a hair, or permitted a sheet to be started.

"You'll take the mast out of her, Don John," said Ned Patterdale, wiping the salt water from his face.

"If I do, I'll put in another," replied Donald. "But you can't snap that stick. The Skylark's mast will go by the board first, and then it will be time enough to look out for ours."

"You have beaten her, Don John," added Ned.

"Not yet. 'There's many a slip between the cup and the lip.'"

"But you are a quarter of a mile ahead of her, at least. It's blowing a gale, and we can't carry all this sail much longer."

"She can carry it as long as the Skylark. When she reefs, we will do the same. I want to show you what the Sea Foam's made of. She is as stiff as a line-of-battle ship."

"But look over to windward, Don John," exclaimed Ned, with evident alarm. "Isn't that a squall?"

"No; I think not. It's only a shower of rain," replied Donald. "There may be a puff of wind in it. If there is, I can touch her up."

"The Skylark has come up into the wind, and dropped her peak," added Norman, considerably excited.

But Donald kept on. In a moment more a heavy shower of rain deluged the deck of the Sea Foam. With it came a smart puff of wind, and the skipper "touched her up;" but it was over in a moment, and the yacht sped on her way towards the goal. Half an hour later she passed the Penobscot, and a gun from her saluted the victor in the exciting race. About four minutes later came the Skylark, which had lost half this time in the squall.

CHAPTER X.

THE LAUNCH OF THE MAUD.

THE heavy rain had driven nearly all the people on board of the Penobscot below, but the judges, clothed in rubber coats, kept the deck, in readiness to take the time of the rival yachts. After the squall, the weather was so thick that both of them were hidden from view. The craft not in the race had anchored near the Penobscot, and on board of all the yachts the interest in the result was most intense.

"I'm afraid it will be no race," said Sam Rodman, who was now the chairman of the judges.

"The commodore will put the Skylark through, whatever the weather," replied Frank Norwood.

"Don John will keep the Sea Foam flying as long as Bob runs the Skylark, you may depend."

"It was quite a little squall that swept across the bay just now," added Rodman. "I hope no accident has happened to them."

"I'll risk the accidents.   I would give a dollar to know which one was ahead."

"Not much doubt on that point."

"I think there is.   Don John generally knows what he is about.   He don't very often say what he can do, but when he does, he means it."

"The commodore is too much for him."

"Perhaps he is, but I have hopes of the Sea Foam.   Don John is building the Maud for me, and I have some interest in this race.   I don't want a yacht that is to be beaten by everything in the fleet.   If the Skylark is too much for the Sea Foam, the chance of the Maud won't be much better."

The judges discussed the merits of the two yachts for half an hour longer, and there was as much difference of opinion among them as among the rest of the spectators of the race.

"There's one of them!" shouted Frank Norwood, as the Sea Foam emerged from the cloud of mist which accompanied the rain.

"Which is it?" demanded Rodman.

"I can't make her out," replied Norwood, for the yacht was over a mile distant.

"But where is the other? One of them is getting badly beaten," added Rodman.

"That must be the Skylark we see."

"I don't believe it is. It is so thick we can't make her out, but her sails look very white. I think it is the Sea Foam."

"There's the other!" exclaimed Norwood, as the Skylark was dimly perceived in the distance.

"She is half a mile astern. It is a bad beat for one of them."

"That's so; and if it is the Sea Foam, I shall want to throw up the contract for the Maud," said Rodman.

"There is one thing about it; both of those craft are good sea boats, and if they can carry whole jib and mainsail in this blow, they are just the right kind of yachts for me. I like an able boat, even if she don't win any prizes. Give me a stiff boat before a fast one."

"I should like to have mine both stiff and fast."

"Look at the Christabel. She went round the course with a reef in the fore and main sails, and was beaten at that," added Norwood. "Here comes the head boat. It is the Skylark, as sure as you live."

"Not much, Frank. Do you see her figure

head? Is it a bird?” demanded Rodman, triumph-
antly.

“It isn’t; that’s a fact.”

“That’s the Sea Foam fast enough.”

This was exciting. news, and Sam Rodman
walked rapidly to the companion-way of the
Penobscot.

“Yachts in sight!” shouted he to the people
below.

“Which is ahead?” asked Mr. Montague.

“The Sea Foam,” replied Rodman.

“I’m so glad!” exclaimed Miss Nellie Patterdale.

Mr. Montague and Captain Patterdale only
laughed, but they were sufficiently interested to
go on deck in spite of the pouring rain, and they
were followed by many others.

“Time!” shouted Sam Rodman, as the gun was
fired.

“Four, thirty-two, ten,” added Frank Norwood; and the figures were entered upon the
schedule.

The Sea Foam passed the judges’ yacht, came
about, and went under her stern.

“The Sea Foam,” shouted Donald.

Though the spectators were not all satisfied with the result, they gave three cheers to the victorious yacht, magnanimously led off by Mr. Montague himself.

"Time!" called Sam, as the Skylark came into the range of the chimney on shore.

"Four, thirty-six, twelve," said Norwood.

The Skylark came about, and passed under the stern of the Penobscot, reporting her name. The judges went below, and figured out the result, by which it appeared that the Sea Foam had beaten the Skylark, after the correction for the three inches' difference in length, by three minutes fifty-nine and four tenths seconds.

Donald was the first to come on board of the Penobscot, and was generously congratulated on his decisive victory, especially by Mr. Montague, the father of the commodore. Robert followed him soon after, and every one was curious to know what he would say and do.

"Don John, you have beaten me," exclaimed he, grasping the hand of Donald. "You have done it fairly and handsomely, and I am ready to give up the first prize to the Sea Foam."

The party in the cabin of the Penobscot heartily applauded the conduct of the commodore.

"You are very kind and generous, Bob," replied Donald, deeply moved by the magnanimity of the commodore.

"When I am whipped, I know it as well as the next man. The silver vase belongs to the Sea Foam."

"Not at all," protested Donald. "This last race was not for the vase, and you won the first one fairly."

"Of course the vase belongs to the commodore," added Rodman. "The judges have already awarded and presented the prizes."

This was the unanimous sentiment of all concerned, and Robert consented to retain the first prize.

"I say, Don John," continued the commodore, removing his wet coat and cap, "I want to have an understanding about the affair. While I own that the Skylark has been beaten, I am not so clear that the Sea Foam is the faster boat of the two."

"I think she is, commodore," laughed Donald; "though I believe I understand your position."

"We made an even thing of it till we came up with Turtle Head—didn't we?"

"Yes, that's so. If either gained anything for the moment, he lost it again," replied Donald.

"Then, if we made exactly the same time to Turtle Head, it seems to me the merits of the two boats are about the same."

"Not exactly, commodore. You forget that the Skylark has to give time to the Sea Foam—one and three-tenths seconds per mile; or about eight seconds from here to the Head."

"That's next to nothing," laughed Robert. "But I was a length ahead of you."

"I let you gain that, so that I could go to windward of you."

"You made your first point by running nearer to the rocks than I like to go, by which you cut off a little of the distance; and inches counted in so close a race."

"That's part of the game in sailing a race."

"I know that, and it's all perfectly fair. I lost half my time when the squall came. I thought it was going to be heavier than it proved to be."

"I threw the Sea Foam up into the wind when it came," said Donald.

"But you didn't drop your peak, and I lost two minutes in doing it. Now, Don John, I can put

12

my finger on the four minutes by which you beat me; and I don't think there is any difference between the two yachts."

"You forget the allowance."

"That's nothing. In all future regattas the result will depend more upon the sailing than upon the boats."

"I think you are quite right, Bob; and the fellow who makes the most mistakes will lose the race. But when the Maud is done she is going to beat you right along, if she has anything like fair play," laughed Donald.

"She may if she can," replied Robert.

The reputation of Ramsay & Son, boat builders, was greatly increased by the result of the race. If Edward Patterdale was a little mortified to have it demonstrated that the Sea Foam had lost the first prize by his own want of skill and tact in sailing her, he was consoled by the fact that Commodore Montague, who had the credit of being the best skipper in Belfast, had been beaten by his yacht. When the shower was over the party went on shore, and Donald hastened to the shop to attend to business. He found that his men had done a good day's work in his absence, and he related to Kennedy all the particulars of the two races.

"It would have been a bad egg for you if you had not been present," said Kennedy, much interested in the story. "In these regattas the sailing of the yacht is half the battle, and these young fellows may ruin your reputation as a boat-builder, if you don't look out for them."

"When I heard Ned Patterdale say he was disappointed in the Sea Foam, I felt that our business was nearly ruined. I think I have done a good thing for our firm to-day."

"So you have, Donald; and when the Maud is finished, I hope you will sail her yourself in the first race she enters."

"I will, if Sam Rodman consents."

Donald paid off his men that night from the money received from Mr. Rodman. The next week he employed another hand, and worked diligently himself. Every day his mother came out to see how the work progressed, as she began to have some hope herself of the success of the firm of Ramsay & Son. Donald paid her all the fees he received for measuring yachts, and thus far this had been enough to support the family. She did not inquire very closely into the financial affairs of the concern, and the active member of it was not very communicative; but she had unbounded confidence in him, and while he was hopeful she was satisfied.

It would be tedious to follow the young builder through all the details of his business. The frame of the Maud was all set up in due time, and then planked. By the first of August, when the vacation at the High School commenced, she was ready to be launched. All the joiner work on deck and in the cabin was completed, and had received two coats of paint. Mr. Rodman had paid a hundred dollars every week on account, which was more than Donald needed to carry on the work, and the affairs of Ramsay & Son were in a very prosperous condition.

On the day of the launch, the Yacht Club attended in a body, and all the young ladies of the High School were present. Miss Maud Rodman, with a bottle in her hand, had consented formally to give her own name to the beautiful craft. Nellie Patterdale was to be on deck with her, attended by Donald and Sam Rodman. The boarding at the end of the shop had been removed, to allow the passage of the yacht into her future element. The ways had been laid down into the water, and well slushed. It was high tide at ten o'clock, and this hour had been chosen for the great event.

"Are you all ready, Mr. Kennedy?" asked Donald.

"All ready," replied the workman.

"Let her slide!" shouted the boat-builder.

A few smart blows with the hammers removed the dog-shores and the wedges, and the Maud began to move very slowly at first. Those on deck were obliged to stoop until the hull had passed out of the shop.

"Now stand up," said Donald, as the yacht passed the end of the shop; and he thrust a long pole, with a flag attached to the end, into the mast hole.

The boat increased her speed as she advanced, and soon struck the water with a splash.

"Now break the bottle, Maud," added Donald.

"I give this yacht the name of Maud," said Miss Rodman, in a loud tone, as she broke the bottle upon the heel of the bowsprit.

"Won't she tip over, Don John?" asked Nellie.

"Not at all; nearly all her ballast has been put

into her, and she will stand up like a queen on the water," answered Donald, proudly, as he realized that the launch was a perfect success.

Loud cheers from the crowd on shore greeted the yacht as she went into the embrace of her chosen element. The ladies waved their handkerchiefs, and the gentlemen their hats. Maud and Nellie returned the salute, and so did Sam Rodman; but Donald was too busy, just then, even to enjoy his triumph. As the hull slid off into the deep water, the boat-builder threw over the anchor, and veered out the cable till her headway was checked. The Maud rested on the water as gracefully as a swan, and the work of the day was done.

Hardly had the yacht brought up at her cable, when the Juno, in which Laud Cavendish had been laying off and on where he could see the launch, ran alongside of her.

"Keep off!" shouted Donald; "you will scrape her sides."

"No; hold on, Don John; I have a cork fender," replied Laud, as he threw his painter on board of the Maud. "Catch a turn—will you?"

"Don't let him come on board, if you can help

it," whispered Nellie Patterdale. "He is a terrible bore."

"I can help it," replied Donald, as, with a
boat-hook he shoved off the bow of the Juno.

Then, for the first time, he observed that Laud
had a passenger, a man whom he remembered to
have seen before, though he did not think where.

"What are you about, Don John?" demanded
Laud.

"Keep off, then," replied Donald. "We don't
want any visitors on board yet. We are going
to haul her up to the wharf at once."

"But I came off to offer the ladies a passage to
the shore," said Laud.

"They don't want any passage to the shore."

"Good morning, Miss Patterdale," added Laud,
as Nellie went to the rail near the Juno. "Allow
me to offer you a place in this boat to convey you
to the shore."

"Thank you, Mr. Cavendish; I intend to remain
where I am," replied she, rather haughtily.

"I shall be happy to take you out to sail, if you
will do me the honor to accompany me; and Miss
Rodman, too, if she will go."

"No, I thank you; I am otherwise engaged,"

answered Nellie, as she retreated to the other side of the yacht.

"I say, Donald, let me come on board," asked Laud, who was desperately bent upon improving his acquaintance with Nellie Patterdale.

"Not now; you can come on board at the wharf."

Donald was resolute, and Laud, angry at his rebuff, filled away.

"Here is a man that wants to see you, Don John," shouted Laud, as he ran his boat up to the Maud again.

"I can't see him now," replied Donald.

Kennedy now came alongside in the skiff, bringing a warp-line from the shore, by which the Maud was hauled up to the wharf. The spectators went on board, and examined the work. Many of them crawled into the cabin and cook-room, and all of them were enthusiastic in their praise, though a few seasoned it with wholesome criticism. Some thought the cabin ought to be longer, evidently believing that it was possible to put a quart of water into a pint bottle; others thought she ought to be rigged as a schooner instead of a sloop, which was a matter of fancy with the owner; but all agreed that she was a beautiful yacht. In honor of the event, and to please the young people, Mr. Rodman had prepared a collation at his house, to which the members of the Yacht Club and others were cordially invited. Kennedy and the other men who worked on the Maud were included in the invitation, and the afternoon was to be a holiday. Laud Cavendish, who had moored the Juno and come on shore, liberally interpreted the invitation to include himself, and joined the party, though he was not a member of the club. Some people have a certain exuberance on the side of their faces, which enables them to do things which others cannot do.

"I want to see you, Don John," said Laud, as the party began to move from the wharf towards the mansion of Mr. Rodman.

"I'll see you this evening," replied Donald, who was anxious to gain a position at the side of Miss Nellie Patterdale.

"That will be too late. You saw the man in the Juno with me—didn't you?" continued Laud, proceeding to open his business.

"I saw him."

"Did you know him?"

"No; though I thought I had seen him before," replied Donald, as they walked along in the rear of the party.

"He is the man who was beaten within an inch of his life over to Lincolnville, a while ago."

"Hasbrook?"

"Yes, his name is Jacob Hasbrook."

"He was with us in the library of Captain Patterdale the day we were there, when the man had a sun-stroke."

"Was he? Well, I don't remember that. Folks say he is a big rascal, and the licking he got was no more than he deserved. He was laid up for a month after it; but now he and the sheriff are trying to find out who did it."

Donald was interested, in spite of himself, and for the time even forgot the pleasant smile of Nellie, which was a great deal for him to forget.

"Has he any idea who it was that beat him?"

"I don't know whether he has or not. He only asks questions, and don't answer any. You know I met you over to Turtle Head the morning after the affair in Lincolnville."

"I remember all about it," answered Donald.

"I saw you in the Juno afterwards. By the

way, Don John, you didn't tell me how you happened to be in the Juno at that time. I don't recollect whether you had her at Turtle Head, or not. I don't think I saw her there, at any rate."

"No matter whether you did or not. Go on with your story, for we are almost to Mr. Rodman's house," replied Donald, impatiently.

"Well, after I left you, I ran over towards Saturday Cove," continued Laud. "You know where that is."

"Of course I do."

This was the place towards which Captain Shivernock had gone in the sail-boat, and where Laud had probably seen him, when he gave him the money paid for the Juno. Laud did not say that this was the time and place he had met the captain, but Donald was entirely satisfied on this point.

"From Saturday Cove I ran on the other tack over to Gilky's Harbor," added Laud.

"Did you see anybody near the cove?"

"I didn't say whether I did or not," replied Laud, after some hesitation, which confirmed Donald's belief that he had met the captain on this occasion. "Never mind that. Off Gilky's Harbor I hailed Tom Reed, who had been a fishing.

It seems that Tom told Hasbrook he saw me that forenoon, and Hasbrook has been to see me half a dozen times about it. I don't know whether he thinks I am the fellow that thrashed him, or not. He has pumped me dry about it. I happened to let on that I saw you, and Hasbrook wants to talk with you."·

By this time they reached Mr. Rodman's house, and to the surprise of Donald, Laud Cavendish coolly walked into the grounds with him.

CHAPTER XI.

THE WHITE CROSS OF DENMARK.

LAUD CAVENDISH was at Donald's side when they entered the grounds of Mr. Rodman, where the tables were spread under the trees in the garden. As the collation was in honor of the launch of the Maud, of course the young boat-builder was a person of no little consequence, and being with him, Laud was permitted to enter the grounds unchallenged; but they soon separated.

Donald was disturbed by what Laud had told him, and he did not wish to answer any questions which might be put to him by Hasbrook, who was evidently working his own case, trying to ascertain who had committed the outrage upon him. He did not wish to tell whom he had seen on that Saturday forenoon, and thus violate the confidence of Captain Shivernock. But he was entirely satisfied that the captain had nothing to do with it, for he had not left his house until after the deed was done, according to the testimony of Sykes and his wife, whom he had separately interviewed. To decline to answer Hasbrook's questions, on the other hand, was to excite suspicion. He could not tell any lies about the case. If he could, it would have been easily managed; as it was, the situation was very awkward. But he had not time to think much of the matter, for one and another began to congratulate him upon the success of the launch, the fine proportions and the workmanship of the Maud. The praise of Captain Patterdale was particularly agreeable to him; but the best news he heard was that Major Norwood intended to have a yacht built for his son, and would probably give the job to Ramsay & Son.

"Well, Don John, you are a real lion," laughed Nellie Patterdale, when, at last, the young boat-builder obtained a place at her side, which had been the objective point with him since he entered the grounds.

"Better be a lion than a bear," replied Donald.

"Everybody says you have built a splendid yacht, and Maud is delighted to have it named after her."

"I think the Sea Foam ought to have been called the Nellie," added Donald.

"Pooh! I asked Ned to call her the Sea Foam."

"If I ever build a yacht on my own account, I shall certainly name her the Nellie Patterdale," continued Donald, though the remark cost him a terrible struggle.

"I thank you, Don John; but I hope you will never build one on your own account, then," answered she, with a slight blush.

"Why, wouldn't you like to have a boat named after you?" asked he, rather taken aback at her reply.

"I shouldn't like to have my whole name given to a boat. It is too long."

"O, well! Then I shall call her the Nellie."

"You are too late, Don John," laughed Laud Cavendish, who was standing within hearing distance, and who now stepped forward, raised his hat, bowed, and smirked. "I have already ordered the painter to inscribe that word on the bows and stern of the Juno, for I never liked her present name."

Nellie blushed deeper than before, but it was with anger this time, though she made no reply to

Laud's impudent remark. At this moment Mr. Rodman invited the party to gather around the tables and partake of the collation.

"Will Miss Patterdale allow me to offer her my arm?" added Laud, as he thrust his elbow up before her.

"No, I thank you," she replied, walking towards the tables, but keeping at Donald's side.

The boat-builder had not the courage to offer her his arm, though some of the sons of the nabobs had done so to the ladies; but he kept at her side. Laud was desperate, for Nellie seemed to be the key of destiny to him. If he could win her heart and hand, or even her hand without the heart, his fortune would be made, and the wealth and social position of which cruel fate had thus far robbed him would be obtained. Though she snubbed him, he could not see it, and would not accept the situation. If Donald had not been there, she would not have declined his offered arm; and he regarded the boat-builder as the only obstacle in his path.

"I wish you had not invited that puppy, Don John," said Nellie, as they moved towards the tables; and there was a snap in her tones which emphasized the remark.

"I didn't invite him," replied Donald, warmly.

"He came in with you, and Mr. Rodman said you must have asked him."

"Indeed, I did not; I had no right to invite him," protested Donald.

Nellie immediately told this to the host of the occasion, and in doing so she left Donald for a moment.

"Why don't you get out of the way, Don John, when you see what I am up to?" said Laud, in a low tone, but earnestly and indignantly, as though Donald had stepped between him and the cheerful destiny in which his imagination revelled.

"What are you up to?"

"I told you before that I liked Nellie, and you are all the time coming between me and her. She would have taken my arm if you had stepped aside."

"I don't choose to step aside," added Donald.

"I want to get in there, Don John," added Laud, in a milder tone.

"Paddle your own canoe."

"You don't care anything about her."

"How do you know I don't?"

"Do you?"

13

"That's my affair."

"She don't care for you."

"Nor you, either."

"Perhaps not now, but I can make it all right with her," said Laud, as he twirled his colored mustache, which he probably regarded as a lady-killer. "Besides, you are not old enough to think of such things yet, Don John."

"Well, I don't think of such things yet," replied Donald, who really spoke only the truth, so far as he was consciously concerned.

"But you ought not to stick by her to-day. You are the boat-builder, and you should bestow your attentions upon Maud Rodman, after whom the yacht was named. She is the daughter of the man who gave you the job. If you will just keep away from Nellie, I can paddle my own canoe, as you say."

"Mr. Cavendish," interposed Mr. Rodman, "I believe you are not a member of the Belfast Yacht Club."

"I am not yet, but I intend to join," replied Laud.

"In the mean time, this occasion is for the members of the club and their friends; and I wish to suggest the propriety of your withdrawing, as I believe you are here without an invitation," added Mr. Rodman.

"I came with Don John," said Laud, rather startled by the plain speech of the host.

"If Don John invited you—"

"I didn't invite him, or any one else. I did not consider that I had any right to do so," protested Donald, as he walked forward and joined Nellie.

Laud could not gainsay this honest avowal; but there was no limit to his wrath at that moment, and he determined to punish the boat-builder for "going back" on him, as he regarded it.

The collation was a sumptuous one, for when Belfast nabobs do anything, they do it. The guests had good appetites, and did abundant justice to the feast. The incident of which Laud Cavendish had been the central figure caused some talk and some laughter.

"He had the impudence to say he was going to name his boat after me," said Nellie Patterdale. "He don't like the name of Juno."

"Does he own the Juno?" asked Captain Patterdale, quietly.

"I suppose he does."

"How is that, Don John?" added the captain.

"Yes, sir, he owns her; Captain Shivernock got tired of the Juno, and Laud bought her."

Captain Patterdale made a note of that piece of information, and regarded it as a clew to assist in the discovery of the tin box, which had not yet been found, though the owner and the deputy sheriff had been looking diligently for it ever since its disappearance.

"What did he pay for her?" inquired Captain Patterdale.

"Three hundred and fifty dollars," answered Donald, who hoped he would not be asked of whom Laud had bought the Juno.

The captain did not ask the question, for it seemed to be self-evident that he had purchased her of Captain Shivernock. Indeed, nothing more was said about the matter. A dance on the shaven lawn followed the collation, and the guests remained until the dews of evening began to fall. Donald walked home with Nellie, and then went to the shop. He expected to find Hasbrook there, but he had returned to Lincolnville. He saw that the sails for the Maud had been sent down during his absence, and on the desk lay the bill for them, enclosed in an envelope, directed to "Messrs. Ramsay & Son." While he was looking at it, Mr. Leach, the sail-maker, entered the shop. He had come to look after his money, for possibly he had not entire confidence in the financial stability of the firm.

"Have you looked over those sails, Don John?" asked Leach.

"Not yet; it is rather too dark to examine them to-night," replied Donald.

"That's the best suit of sails I ever made," added the sail-maker. "You said you wanted the best that could be had."

"I did." And Donald unrolled them. "They look like a good job."

"If they are not as good as anything that ever went on a boat, I'll make you another suit for nothing. I was in hopes you would look them over to-night. I don't want to trouble you, Don John, but I'm a little short of money. Captain Patterdale has a mortgage on my house, and I like to pay the interest on it the day it is due. You said you would let me have the money when the sails were delivered."

"And so I will."

"If they are not all right, I will make them so," added Leach. "I should like to pay the captain my interest money to-night, if I can."

"You can. I will go into the house and get the money."

Donald went to his room in the cottage, and took from their hiding-place the bills which had been paid to him by Laud Cavendish for the Juno. Without this he had not enough to pay the sail-maker. He did not like to use this money, for he was not fully satisfied that Laud would not get into trouble on account of it, or that he might not himself have some difficulty with Captain Shiver-nock. He feared that he should be called upon to refund this money; but Mr. Rodman would pay him another instalment of the price of the Maud in a few days, and he should then be in condition to meet any demand upon him. Laud had paid him seven fifty-dollar bills, and he put them in his pocket. As he passed through the kitchen, he lighted the lantern, and returned to the shop.

"I didn't mean to dun you up so sharp for this bill," said Leach; "but I haven't a dollar in my pocket at this minute, and I am very anxious to be punctual in the payment of my interest."

"It's all right; I had as lief pay it now as at any other time. In fact, I like to pay up as soon as the work is done," replied Donald, as he handed the sail-maker three of the fifty-dollar bills, which was the price agreed upon for the sails, five in number.

Leach looked carefully at each of the bills. All of them were quite new and fresh, and one was peculiar enough to attract the attention of any one through whose hands it might pass. It was just like the others, but at some period, not very remote in its history, it had been torn into four parts. It might have been in a sheet of note paper, torn up by some one who did not know the bill was between the leaves. It had been mended with two narrow slips of thin, white paper, extending across the length and width of the bill, like the horizontal white cross on the flag of Denmark.

"That bill has been in four pieces," said Leach, as he turned it over and examined it; "but I suppose it is good."

"If it is not, I will give you another for it," answered Donald.

"It is all here; so I think it is all right. I wonder who tore it up."

"I don't know; it was so when I took it."

"I am very much obliged to you, Don John; and the next time I make a suit of sails for you, you needn't pay me till you get ready," said the sail-maker, as he put the money in his wallet.

"I didn't pay for this suit till I got ready," laughed the boat-builder; "and when you get up another, I hope I shall be able to pay you the cash for them."

Leach left the shop a happy man; for most men are cheerful when they have plenty of money in their pocket. He was more especially happy because, being an honest man, he was able now to pay the interest on the mortgage note on the day it was due. He had worked half the night before in order to finish the sails, so that he might get the money to pay it. With a light step, therefore, he walked to the elegant mansion of Captain Patterdale, and rang the bell at the library door. There was a light in the room, which indicated that the captain was at home. He was admitted by the nabob himself, who answered his own bell at this door.

"I suppose you thought I wasn't going to pay my interest on the day it was due," said Leach, with a cheerful smile.

The Sail-maker's Bill. Page 199.

"On the contrary, I didn't think anything at all about it," replied Captain Patterdale. "I was not even aware that your interest was due to-day."

"I came pretty near not paying it, for work has been rather slack this season; but the firm of Ramsay & Son helped me out by paying me promptly for the sails I made for the Maud."

"Ramsay & Son is a great concern," laughed the nabob.

"It pays promptly; and that's more than all of them do," added Leach, drawing his wallet from his pocket.

"I haven't your note by me, Mr. Leach," said Captain Patterdale; but he did not consider it necessary to state that the important document was at that moment in the tin box, wherever the said tin box might be. "I will give you a receipt for the amount you pay, and indorse it upon the note when I have it."

"All right, captain."

"Do you know how much the interest is? I am sure I have forgotten," added the rich man.

"I ought to know. I have had to work too hard to get the money in time to forget how much it was. It is just seventy dollars," answered Leach.

"You needn't pay it now, if you are short."

"I'm not short now. I'm flush, for which I thank Don John," said the sail-maker, as he placed two of the fifty-dollar bills on the desk, at which the captain was writing the receipt.

The uppermost of the two bills was the mended one, for Leach thought if there was any doubt in regard to this, it ought to be known at once. If the nabob would take it, the matter was settled. Captain Patterdale wrote the receipt, and did not at once glance at the money.

"There's a hundred, captain," added the sail-maker.

The rich man picked up the bills, and turned over the upper one. If he did not start, it was not because he was not surprised. He was utterly confounded when he saw that bill, and his thoughts flashed quickly through his mind. But he did not betray his thoughts or his emotions, quick as were the former, and intense as were the latter. He took up the mended bill, and looked it over several times.

"That's the white cross of Denmark," said he, suppressing his emotions.

"Isn't the bill good?" asked the sail-maker.

"Good as gold for eighty-eight cents on a dollar," replied the captain.

"Then it is not good," added Leach, who did not quite comprehend the nabob's mathematics.

"Yes, it is."

"But you say it is worth only eighty-eight cents on a dollar."

"That is all any paper dollar is worth when gold is a little rising fourteen per cent. premium. The bill is perfectly good, in spite of the white cross upon it. You want thirty dollars change."

The captain counted out this sum, and handed it to the debtor.

"If the bill isn't good, I can give you another," replied Leach, as he took the money.

"It is a good bill, and I prefer it to any other for certain reasons of my own. It has the white cross of Denmark upon it; at least, the white bars on this bill remind me of the flag of that nation."

"It's like a flag—is it?" added the sail-maker, who did not understand the rich man's allusion.

"Like the flag of Denmark. I made a voyage to Copenhagen once, and this bill reminds me of the merchant's flag, which has a couple of white bars across a red ground. Where did you say you got this bill, Mr. Leach?"

"Don John gave it to me, not half an hour ago."

"It has been torn into quarters some time, and the pieces put together again. Did Don John mend the bill himself?"

"No, sir; he says the bill is just as it was when he received it. I looked at it pretty sharp when I took it; but he said if it wasn't good, he would give me another."

"It is perfectly good. Did he tell you where he got the bill?" asked Captain Patterdale, manifesting none of the emotion which agitated him.

"No, sir; he did not. I didn't ask him. If it makes any difference, I will do so."

"It makes no difference whatever. It is all right, Mr. Leach."

The sail-maker folded up his receipt, and left the library. He went home with eighty dollars in his pocket, entirely satisfied with himself, with the nabob, and especially with the firm of Ramsay & Son. He did not care a straw about the white cross of Denmark, so long as the bill was good. Captain Patterdale was deeply interested in the bill which bore this mark, and possibly he expected to conquer by this sign. He was not so much interested in the bill because he had made a voyage up the Baltic and seen the white cross there, as because he had seen it on a bill in that tin box. He was not only interested, but he was anxious, for the active member of the firm of Ramsay & Son seemed to be implicated in a very unfortunate and criminal transaction.

More than once Captain Patterdale had observed the pleasant relations between Don John and his fair daughter. As Nellie was a very pretty girl, intelligent, well educated, and agreeable, and in due time would be the heiress of a quarter or a half million, as the case might be, he was rather particular in regard to the friendships she contracted with the young gentlemen of the city. Possibly he did not approve the intimacy between them. But whatever opinions he may have entertained in regard to the equality of social relations between his daughter and the future partner of her joys and sorrows, we must do him the justice to say that he preferred honor and honesty to wealth and position in the gentleman whom Nellie might choose for her life companion. The suspicion, or rather the conviction, forced upon him by "the white cross of Denmark," that Donald was neither honest nor honorable, was vastly more painful than the fact that he was poor, and was the son of a mere ship carpenter.

Certainly Nellie did like the young man, though, as she was hardly more than a child, it might be a fancy that would pass away when she realized the difference between the daughter of a nabob and the son of a ship carpenter.   While he was thinking of the subject, Nellie entered the library, as she generally did when her father was alone there. She was his only confidant in the house in the matter of the tin box, and he determined to talk with her about the painful discovery he had just made.

CHAPTER XII.

DONALD ANSWERS QUESTIONS.

"WELL, Nellie, did you have a good time to-day?" asked Captain Patterdale, as his daughter seated herself near his desk.

"I did; a capital time. Everybody seemed to enjoy it," replied she.

"But some seemed to enjoy it more than others," added the captain, with a smile.

"Now, father, you have something to say," said she, with a blush. "I wish you would say it right out, and not torment me for half an hour, trying to guess what it is."

"Of course, if I hadn't anything to say, I should hold my tongue," laughed her father.

"Everybody don't."

"But I do."

"Do you think I enjoyed the occasion more than any one else, father?"

"I thought you were one of the few who enjoyed it most."

"Perhaps I was; but what have I done?"

"Done?"

"What terrible sin have I committed now?"

"None, my child."

"But you are going to tell me that I have sinned against the letter of the law of propriety, or something of that kind. This is the way you always begin."

"Then this time is an exception to all other times, for I haven't a word of fault to find with you."

"I am so glad! I was trying to think what wicked thing I had been doing."

"Nothing, child. Don John seemed to be supremely happy this afternoon."

"I dare say he was; but the firm of Ramsay & Son had a successful launch, and Don John had compliments enough to turn the head of any one with a particle of vanity in his composition."

"No doubt of it; and I suppose you were not behind the others in adding fuel to the flame."

"What flame, father?"

"The flame of vanity."

"On the contrary, I don't think I uttered a single compliment to him."

"It was hardly necessary to utter it; but if you had danced with him only half as often, it would have flattered his vanity less."

"How could I help it, when he asked me? There were more gentlemen than ladies present, and I did not like to break up the sets," protested Nellie.

"Of course not; but being the lion of the occasion, don't you think he might have divided himself up a little more equitably?"

"I don't know; but I couldn't choose my own partner," replied Nellie, her cheeks glowing.

"You like Don John very well?"

"I certainly do, father," replied she, honestly. "Don't you?"

"Perhaps it don't make so much difference whether I like him or not."

"You have praised him to the skies, father. You said he was a very smart boy; and not one in a hundred young fellows takes hold of business with so much energy and good judgment. I am sure, if you had not said so much in his favor, I

14

shouldn't have thought half so much of him," argued Nellie.

"I don't blame you for thinking well of him, my child," interposed her father. "I only hope you are not becoming too much interested in him."

"I only like him as a good-hearted, noble fellow," added Nellie, with a deeper blush than before, for she could not help understanding just what her father meant.

"He appears to be a very good-hearted fellow now; but he is young, and has not yet fully developed his character. He may yet turn out to be a worthless fellow, dissolute and dishonest," continued the captain.

"Don John!" exclaimed Nellie, utterly unwilling to accept such a supposition.

"Even Don John. I can recall more than one young man, who promised as well as he does, that turned out very badly; and men fully developed in character, sustaining the highest reputations in the community, have been detected in the grossest frauds. I trust Don John will realize the hopes of his friends; but we must not be too positive."

"I can't believe that Don John will ever become a bad man," protested Nellie.

"We don't know. 'Put not your trust in princes,' in our day and nation, might read, 'Put not your trust in young men.' "

"Why do you say all this, father?" asked Nellie, anxiously. "Has Don John done anything wrong; or is he suspected of doing anything wrong?"

"He is at least suspected," replied Captain Patterdale.

"Why, father!"

"You need not be in haste to condemn him, or even to think ill of him, Nellie."

"I certainly shall not."

"There is the white cross of Denmark," added the captain, holding up the bank bill which had told him such a terrible story about the boat-builder.

"What is it, father? It looks like a bank note."

"It is; but there is the white cross of Denmark on it."

"I don't understand what you mean."

"I only mean that these white slips of paper make the bill look like the flag of Denmark."

Nellie took the bill and examined it.

"It has been torn into four pieces and mended," said she.

"That is precisely how it happens to be the white cross of Denmark. Do you think, if you had ever seen that bill before, you would recognize it again, if it fell into your hands?" added the captain.

"Certainly I should."

"Well, it has been in my hands before. Do you remember the day that Michael had the sunstroke?"

"'Yes, sir; and your tin box disappeared that day."

"Precisely so; and this bill was in that tin box. Jacob Hasbrook, of Lincolnville, paid me a note. I put the money in the box, intending to take it over to the bank before night, and deposit it the next day. I looked at the bill when I counted the money, and I spoke to Hasbrook about it. I called it the white cross of Denmark then."

"Where did you get it now?" inquired Nellie, her heart in her throat with anxiety.

"Mr. Leach, the sail-maker, paid it to me just before you came into the library."

"Mr. Leach!" exclaimed she, permitting herself to be cheered by a ray of hope that her father was not working up a case against Donald Ramsay.

"Yes; you remember who were in the library on the day I lost the tin box."

"I remember very well; for all of you went out and carried Michael into the house. Besides we talked about the box ever so long. You asked me who had been in the library while you were up stairs; and I told you Mr. Hasbrook, Laud Cavendish, and Don John."

"Precisely so; I remember it all very distinctly. Now, one of the bills that was in that box comes back to me."

"But it was paid to you by Mr. Leach."

"It was; but he had it from Don John half an hour before he paid it to me."

"Why, father!" exclaimed Nellie, with real anguish; for even a suspicion against Donald was a shock to her. "I can never believe it!"

"I don't wish you to believe anything yet; but you may as well be prepared for anything an investigation may disclose."

"That Don John should steal!" ejaculated Nellie. "Why, we all considered him the very soul of honor!"

"You are getting along faster than I do with your conclusions, child," added Captain Patterdale. "A suspicion is not proof. The bill came from him, beyond a doubt. But something can be said in his favor, besides the statement that his character is excellent. Of the three persons who were in the library that day, two of them had wagons on the street. It does not seem probable that Don John walked through the city with that tin box in his hand. If he did, some one must have seen it. Of course he would not have carried it openly, while it could easily have been concealed in the wagon of Hasbrook or Laud Cavendish."

"Certainly; if Don John had taken it, he would not have dared to carry it through the streets," added Nellie, comforted by the suggestion.

"Again, if he had stolen this white cross of Denmark, he would not have been likely to pass it off here in Belfast," continued the captain; "for he is sharp enough to see that it would be identified as soon as it appeared. Very likely Mr. Leach told him he intended to pay me some money, and he surely would not have allowed the bill to come back to me."

"I know he didn't do it," cried Nellie, with enthusiasm.

"You are too fast again, child. It is possible that he did, however improbable it may seem now, for rogues often make very silly blunders. Is Edward in the house?"

"I think so; he was reading the *Age* when I came in."

"Tell him to go down and ask Don John to come up and see me. We will have the matter cleared up before we sleep. But, Nellie, don't tell Edward what I want to see Don John for. Not a word about that to any one. By keeping my own counsel, I may get at the whole truth; whereas the thief, if he gets wind of what I am doing, may cover his tracks or run away."

"I will be very discreet, father," replied Nellie, as she left the library.

In a few moments she returned.

"He has gone, father; though he is very tired," said she.

"I suppose he is; but I don't want to believe that Don John is a thief even over one night," replied the captain.

"He asked me what you wanted of Don John; but I didn't tell him."

The father and daughter discussed the painful

suspicion until Donald arrived, and entered the library with Edward. A conversation on indifferent topics was continued for some time, and the boat-builder wondered if he had been sent for to talk about the launch of the Maud, which was now an old story.

"How is the wind, Edward?" asked Captain Patterdale.

'Sou'-sou'-west, half west," laughed Edward, who understood precisely what his father meant by his question; and bidding Donald good night, he left the library, without the formality of saying he would go and see which way the wind was.

"You know which way the wind is, Nellie; and so you need not leave," added the captain, as she rose from her seat to follow the example of her brother.

"So did Ned, for he told you," she answered.

"And you heard him, and know also."

When Captain Patterdale had private business with a visitor, and he wished any member of his own family to retire, he always asked which way the wind was.

"Don John, you had a great success in the launch of the Maud to-day," said the nabob; but

as the same thing had been said half a dozen times
before since the boat-builder entered the room, it
was hardly to be regarded as an original idea; and
Donald was satisfied that the launch was not the
business upon which he had been sent for.

"Yes, sir; we got her off very well," he replied.
"I was sorry I couldn't launch her with the mast
stepped, so as to dress her in the colors."

"In that case, you would have needed the flags
of all nations. I have them, and will lend them
to you any time when you wish to make a sensation."

"Thank you, sir."

"I have here the white cross of Denmark,"
added the captain, holding up the mended bill.

"A fifty-dollar white-cross," laughed Donald.
"I have seen it before."

"This bill?"

"Yes, sir; I paid it to Mr. Leach for the Maud's
sails since dark," answered Donald, so squarely,
that the nabob could not help looking at his daughter and smiling.

"He said you paid promptly, which is a solid
virtue in a business man. By the way, Don John,
you will be out of work as soon as the Maud is
finished."

"I hope to have another yacht to build by that time, especially if the Maud does well."

"I wanted to say a word to you about that, and tell you some good news, Don John," continued Captain Patterdale, as calmly as though he had no interest whatever in the mended bill. "I had a long talk with Mr. Norwood this afternoon. He says he shall give you the job if the Maud sails as well as the Skylark or the Sea Foam. He don't insist that she shall beat them."

"But I expect she will do it; if she don't I shall be disappointed," added Donald.

"Don't expect too much, Don John. I thought you would sleep better if you knew just how Mr. Norwood stood on this question."

"I shall, sir; and I am very much obliged to you."

"Do you think you will make any money on the building of the Maud?" asked the nabob.

"Yes, sir. I think I shall do pretty well with her."

"You seem to have money enough to pay your bills as you go along. Did Mr. Rodman pay you this bill?" inquired the captain, as he held up the white cross again.

"No, sir; he did not. I have had that bill in the house for some time," replied Donald.

"Are you so flush as that?"

"Yes, sir; I had considerable cash in the house."

"Your father left something, I suppose."

"Yes, sir; but he never had that bill and the other two I paid Mr. Leach," replied Donald; and he could not help thinking all the time that they were a part of the sum Laud Cavendish had paid him for the Juno, under promise not to say where he got it, if everything was all right.

Though the boat-builder was a square young man, he could not help being somewhat embarrassed, for his sense of honor did not permit him to violate the confidence of any one.

"If it is a fair question, Don John, where did you get this bill?" asked the captain.

Donald thought it was hardly a fair question under the circumstances, and he made no answer, for he was thinking how he could get along without a lie, and still say nothing about Laud's connection with the bill, for that would expose Captain Shivernock.

"You don't answer me, Don John," added the nabob, mildly.

"I don't like to tell," replied Donald.

"Why not?"

"I promised not to do so."

"You promised not to tell where you got this money?"

Poor Nellie was almost overwhelmed by these answers on the part of Donald, and her father began to have some painful doubts.

"I did, sir; that is, I promised not to tell if everything about the money was all right."

"If you don't tell where you got the money, how are you to know whether everything is all right or not?" demanded Captain Patterdale, in sharper tones than he had yet used.

"Well, I don't know," answered the boat-builder, not a little confused, and sadly troubled by the anxious expression on Miss Nellie's pretty face.

Perhaps her father, who understood human nature exceedingly well, had required her to remain in the library during this interview, for a purpose; but whether he did or not, Donald was really more concerned about her good opinion than he was about that of any other person in the world, unless it was his mother. He was conscious that he was not making a good appearance; and under the sad gaze of those pretty eyes, he was determined to redeem himself.

"You ought not to make such promises, Don John," said the captain; and this time he spoke quite sternly.

"You have that bill, sir. Is there anything wrong about it?" asked Donald.

"Yes."

"Then my promise covers nothing. Laud Cavendish paid me that bill," added the boat-builder.

"Laud Cavendish!" exclaimed Nellie.

Her father shook his head, to intimate that she was to say nothing.

"Laud Cavendish gave you this bill?" repeated the captain.

"Yes, sir, and six more just like it; only the others were not mended. I paid Mr. Leach three of them, and here are the other four," said Donald, producing his wallet, and taking from it the four bills, which he had not returned to their hiding-place in the bureau.

Captain Patterdale examined them, and compared them with the two in his possession. They looked like the bills he had deposited in the tin box, when Hasbrook paid him the thirteen hundred and fifty dollars and interest. Twelve of the bills which made up this sum were fifties, nearly new; the balance was in hundreds, and smaller notes, older, more discolored, and worn.

"Laud Cavendish paid you three hundred and fifty dollars, then?" continued the nabob.

"Yes, sir; just that. But what is there wrong about it?" asked Donald, trembling with emotion, when he realized what a scrape he had got into.

"Following your example, Don John, I shall for the present decline to answer," replied the captain. "If you don't know—"

"I don't!" protested Donald, earnestly.

"If you don't know, I thank God; and I congratulate you that you don't know."

"I haven't the least idea."

"Of course, if you don't wish to answer any question I may ask, you can decline to answer, as I do, Don John."

"I am entirely willing to answer any and every question that concerns me."

"As you please; but you can't be called upon to say anything that will criminate yourself."

"Criminate myself, sir!" exclaimed Donald, aghast. "I haven't done anything wrong."

"I don't say that you have, Don John; more than that, I don't believe you have; but if you answer any question of mine, you must do it of your own free will and accord."

"I will, sir."

"For what did Laud Cavendish pay you three hundred and fifty dollars?"

"For the Juno," replied Donald, promptly.

"I did not know he owned the Juno."

"He said he did to-day; at least, he said he was going to change her name," added Nellie.

"The fact that I did not know it doesn't prove that it was not so. You sold the Juno to Laud, did you, Don John?"

"I did, sir."

"Did you own the Juno?"

"Yes, sir."

"Did you buy her of Captain Shivernock?"

"No, sir; I did not buy her; he made me a present of her."

"A present!"

"Yes, sir; he got disgusted with her, and gave her to me. I could not afford to keep her, and sold her to Laud Cavendish."

"Gave her to you! That's very strange."

"But Captain Shivernock is a very strange man."

"None will dispute that," replied Captain Patterdale, with a smile and a shrug of the shoulders. "That man throws away his property with utter recklessness; and I should not be surprised if he ended his life in the almshouse. I will not ask any explanation of the conduct of Captain Shivernock. Laud Cavendish is not a man of means. Did he tell you, Donald, where he got his money to buy a boat worth three hundred and fifty dollars?"

"He did, sir, and explained the matter so that I was satisfied; for I would not sell him the Juno till he convinced me that there was no hitch about the money."

"Well, where did he get it?"

"I don't feel at liberty to tell, sir; for he told me it was a great secret, which did not affect him, but another person. I inquired into the matter myself, and was satisfied it was all right."

"I am afraid you have been deceived, Don John; but I am convinced you have done no wrong yourself—at least, not intentionally. Secrets are dangerous; and when people wish you to conceal

anything, you may generally be sure there is something wrong somewhere, though it may look all right to you. I have no more questions to ask to-night, Don John; but I may wish to see you again in regard to this subject. I must see Mr. Laud Cavendish next."

Donald declared that he was ready to give all the information in his power; and after a little chat with Nellie, he went home, with more on his mind than had troubled him before, since he could remember.

15

CHAPTER XIII.

MOONLIGHT ON THE JUNO.

DONALD felt that he was in hot water, in spite of the assurance of Captain Patterdale that he believed him innocent of all wrong, and he was sorry that he had made any bargains, conditional or otherwise, with Captain Shivernock or Laud Cavendish. The nabob would not tell him what was wrong, and he could not determine whether Laud or some other person had stolen the money. He went into the house on his return from the elegant mansion. His mother had gone to watch with a sick neighbor, though his sister Barbara was sewing in the front room.

Donald was troubled, not by a guilty conscience, but by the fear that he had innocently done wrong in concealing his relations with Captain Shivernock and with Laud Cavendish. Somehow the case looked different now from what it had before.

Laud had told where he got his money, and given a good reason, as it seemed to him at the time, for concealment; but why the strange man desired secrecy he was utterly unable to imagine. He almost wished he had told Captain Patterdale all about his meeting with Captain Shivernock on Long Island, and asked his advice. It was not too late to do so now. Donald was so uneasy that he could not sit in the house, and went out doors. He walked about the beach for a time, and then sat down in front of the shop to think the matter over again.

Suddenly, while he was meditating in the darkness, he saw the trunk lights of the Maud illuminated, as though there was a fire in her cabin. He did not wait to study the cause, but jumping into his skiff, he pushed off, and sculled with all his might towards the yacht. He was mad and desperate, for the Maud was on fire! He leaped on board, with the key of the brass padlock which secured the cabin door in his hand; but he had scarcely reached the deck before he saw a man on the wharf retreating from the vicinity of the yacht. Then he heard the flapping of a sail on the other side of the pier; but he could not spend an instant

in ascertaining who the person was. He opened
the cabin door, and discovered on the floor a pile
of shavings in flames. Fortunately there was a
bucket in the standing-room, with which he dashed
a quantity of water upon the fire, and quickly
extinguished it. All was dark again; but to make
sure, Donald threw another pail of water on the
cabin floor, and then it was not possible for the
fire to ignite again.

Although the deck had been swept clean before
the launch, the side next to the wharf was littered
with shavings, and a basket stood there, in which
they had been brought on board, for it was still
half full. Donald found that one of the trunk
lights had been left unfastened, in the hurry and
excitement of attending the festival at Mr. Rodman's house. Through the aperture the incendiary had stuffed the shavings, and dropped a card
of lighted matches upon them, for he saw the rem-
nants of it when he threw on the first water. Who
had done this outrageous deed? Donald sprang
upon the wharf as he recalled the shadowy form
and the flapping sail he had seen. Leaping upon
the pier, he rushed over to the other side, where
he discovered a sail-boat slowly making her way,
in the gentle breeze, out of the dock.

Beyond a peradventure, the boat was the Juno. Her peculiar rig enabled him readily to identify her. Was Laud Cavendish in her, and was he wicked enough to commit such an act? Donald returned to the Maud to assure himself that there was no more fire in her. He was satisfied that the yacht was not injured, for he had extinguished the fire before the shavings were well kindled. He fastened the trunk lights securely, locked the cabin door, and taking possession of the basket, he embarked in his skiff again. Sculling out beyond the wharf, he looked for the Juno. The wind was so light she made but little headway, and was standing off shore with the breeze nearly aft. It was Laud's boat, but it might not be Laud in her. Why should the wretch attempt to burn the Maud?

Then the scene in Mr. Rodman's garden, when Laud had been invited to leave, came to his mind, and Donald began to understand the matter. While he was thinking about it, the moon came out from behind a cloud which had obscured it, and cast its soft light upon the quiet bay, silvering the ripples on its waters with a flood of beauty.

Donald glanced at the basket in the skiff, still half filled with shavings. It was Laud's basket, beyond a doubt, for he had often seen it when the owner came down to the shore to embark in his boat. The initials of his father's name, "J. C.," were daubed upon the outside of it, for there is sometimes as much confusion in regard to the ownership of baskets as of umbrellas. Donald was full of excitement, and full of wrath; and as soon as he got the idea of the guilty party through his head, he sculled the skiff with all the vigor of a strong arm towards the Juno, easily overhauling her in a few moments. He was so excited that he dashed his skiff bang into the Juno, to the serious detriment of the white paint which covered her side.

"What are you about, Don John?" roared Laud Cavendish, who had seen the approaching skiff, but had not chosen to hail her.

"What are you about?" demanded Donald, answering the question with another, Yankee fashion, as he jammed his boat-hook into the side of the Juno, and drew the skiff up to the yacht, from which it had receded.

Taking the painter, he jumped on the forward deck of the Juno, with the boat-hook still in his hand.

"What do you mean by smashing into me in that kind of style, and jabbing your boat-hook into the side of my boat?" cried Laud, as fiercely as he could pitch his tones, though there seemed to be a want of vim to them.

"What do you mean by setting the Maud afire?" demanded Donald. "That's what I want to know."

"Who set her afire?" replied Laud, in rather hollow tones.

"You did, you miserable spindle-shanks!"

"I didn't set her afire, Don John," protested Laud.

"Yes, you did! I can prove it, and I will prove it, too."

"You are excited, Don John. You don't know what you are talking about."

"I think I do, and I'll bet you'll understand it, too, if there is any law left in the State of Maine."

"What do you mean by that?"

"I mean what I say, and say what I mean."

"I haven't been near the Maud."

"Yes, you have! Didn't I see you sneaking across the wharf? Didn't I see your mainsail alongside the pier? You can't humbug me. I know a pint of soft soap from a pound of cheese," rattled Donald, who could talk very fast when he was both excited and enraged; and Laud's tongue was no match for his member.

"I tell you, I haven't been near the Maud."

"Don't tell me! I saw it all; I have two eyes that I wouldn't sell for two cents apiece; and I'll put you over the road at a two-forty gait."

Laud saw that it was no use to argue the point, and he held his peace, till the boat-builder had exhausted his rhetoric, and his stock of expletives.

"What did you do it for, Laud?" asked he, at last, in a comparatively quiet tone.

"I have told you a dozen times I didn't do it," replied the accused. "You talk so fast I can't get a word in edgeways."

"It's no use for you to deny it," added Don John.

"Do you think I'd burn your yacht?"

"Yes, I do; and I know you tried to do it. If I hadn't been over by the shop, you would have done it."

"I didn't do it, I repeat. Do you think I would lie about it? Do you think I have no sense of honor about me!"

Don John visits the Juno.   Page 230.

"Confound your honor!" sneered Donald.

"Don't insult me. When you assail my honor, you touch me in a tender place."

"In a soft place, and that's in your head."

"Be careful, Don John. I advise you not to wake a sleeping lion."

"A sleeping jackass!"

"I claim to be a gentleman, and my honor is my capital stock in life."

"You have a very small capital to work on, then."

"I warn you to be cautious, Don John. My honor is all I have to rest upon in this world."

"It's a broken reed. I wouldn't give a cent's worth of molasses candy for the honor of a fellow who would destroy the property of another, because he got mad with him."

In spite of his repeated warnings, Laud Cavendish was very forbearing, though Donald kept the boat-hook where it would be serviceable in an emergency.

"No, Don John, I did not set the Maud afire. Though you went back on me this afternoon, and served me a mean and shabby trick, I wouldn't do such a thing as burn your property."

"Who went back on you?" demanded Donald.

"You did; when you could have saved me from being driven out of the garden, you took the trouble to say, you did not invite me," replied Laud, reproachfully.

"I didn't invite you; and I had no right to invite you."

"No matter for that; if you had just said that your friend, Mr. Cavendish, had come in with you it would have been all right."

"My friend, Mr. Cavendish!" repeated Donald, sarcastically. "I didn't know I had any such friend."

"I didn't expect that of you, after what I had done for you, Don John."

"Spill her on that tack! You never did anything for me."

"I took that boat off your hands, and I suppose you got a commission for selling her. Wasn't that doing something for you?"

"No!" protested Donald.

"I have always used you well, and done more for you than you know of. You wouldn't have got the job to build the Maud if it hadn't been for me. I spoke a good word for you to Mr. Rodman," whined Laud.

"You!" exclaimed Donald, disgusted with this ridiculous pretension. "If you said anything to Mr. Rodman about it, I wonder he didn't give the job to somebody else."

"You think I have no influence, but you are mistaken; and if you insist on quarrelling with me, you will find out, when it is too late, what folks think of me."

"They think you are a ninny; and when they know what you did to-night, they will believe you are a knave," replied Donald. "You didn't cover your tracks so that I couldn't find them; and I can prove all I say. I didn't think you were such a rascal before."

"You won't make anything out of that sort of talk with me, Don John," said Laud, mildly. "You provoke me to throw you overboard, but I don't want to hurt you."

"I'll risk your throwing me overboard. I can take care of myself."

"I said I didn't want to hurt you, and I don't. I didn't set your boat afire; I wouldn't do such a thing."

"You can tell that to Squire Peters to-morrow."

"You don't mean to say that you will prosecute me, Don John?"

"Yes; I do mean it."

"I came down from the harbor, and tacked between those two wharves," explained Laud. "I was standing off on this tack when you bunted your skiff into me. That's all I know about it."

"But I saw you on the wharf. No matter; we won't argue the case here," said Donald, as he made a movement to go into his skiff.

"Hold on, Don John. I want to talk with you a little."

"What about?"

"Two or three things. I am going off on a long cruise in a day or two. I think I shall go as far as Portland, and try to get a situation in a store there."

"I don't believe you will have a chance to go to Portland, or anywhere else, unless it's Thomaston, where the state prison is located."

"I didn't think you would be so rough on me, Don John. I didn't set your boat afire; but I can see that it may go hard with me, because I happened to be near the wharf at the time."

"You will find that isn't the worst of it," added Donald.

"What is the worst of it?"

"Never mind; I'll tell Squire Peters to-morrow, when we come together."

"Don't go to law about it, Don John; for though I didn't do it, I don't want to be hauled up for it. Even a suspicion is sometimes damaging to the honor of a gentleman."

"You had better come down from that high horse, and own up that you set the Maud afire."

"Will you agree not to prosecute, if I do?" asked Laud.

Donald, after his anger subsided, thought more about the "white cross of Denmark" than he did about the fire; for the latter had done him no damage, while the former might injure his character which he valued more than his property.

"I will agree not to prosecute, if you will answer all my questions," he replied; but I confess that it was an error on the part of the young man.

Donald fastened the painter of his skiff at the stern, and took a seat in the standing-room of the Juno.

"I will tell you all I know, if you will keep me out of the courts," added Laud, promptly.

"Why did you set the Maud afire?"

"Because I was mad, and meant to get even

with you for what you did at Rodman's this afternoon. You might do me a great service, Don John, if you would. I like Nellie Patterdale; I mean, I'm in love with her. I don't believe I can live without her."

"I'll bet you'll have to," interposed Donald, indignantly.

"You don't know what it is to love, Don John."

"I don't want to know yet awhile; and I think you had better live on a different sort of grub. What a stupid idea, for a fellow like you to think of such a girl as Nellie Patterdale!"

"Is it any worse for me to think of her, than it is for you to do so?" asked Laud.

"I never thought of her in any such way as that. We went to school together, and have always been good friends; that's all."

"That's enough," sighed Laud. "I actually suffer for her sake. If the quest were hopeless," Laud read novels—"I think I should drown myself."

"You had better do it right off, then," added Donald.

"You can pity me, Don John, for I am miserable. Day and night I think only of her. My feelings have made me almost crazy, and I hardly knew what I was about when I applied the incendiary torch to the Maud.''

''I thought it was a card of friction matches.''

''The world will laugh and jeer at me for loving one above my station; but love makes us equals.''

''Perhaps it does when the love is on both sides,'' added the practical boat-builder.

''But I think I am fitted to adorn a higher station than that in which I was born.''

''If so, you will rise like a stick of timber forced under the water; but it strikes me that you have begun in the wrong way to figure for a rise.''

''But I wish to rise only for Nellie's sake. You can help me, Don John; you can take me into her presence, where I can have the opportunity to win her affection.''

''I guess not, Laud. Shall I tell you what she said to me this afternoon?''

''Tell me all.''

''She said you were an impudent puppy, and she was sorry I invited you.''

''Did she say that?'' asked Laud, looking up to the cold, pale moon.

''She did; and I was obliged to tell her that I didn't invite you.''

"Perhaps I have been a fool," mused the lover.

"There's no doubt of it. Nellie Patterdale dislikes, and even despises you. I have heard her say as much, in so many words. That ought to comfort you, and convince you that it is no use to fish any longer in those waters."

"Possibly you are right; but it is only because she does not know me. If she only knew me better—"

"She would dislike and despise you still more," said Donald, sharply. "If she only knew that you set the Maud afire, she would love you as a homeless dog likes the brickbats that are thrown at him."

"You will not tell her that, Don John?"

"I will not tell her, or any one else, if you behave yourself. Now I want to ask some more questions."

"Go on, Don John."

"Where did you get the money you paid for the Juno?" demanded Donald, with energy.

"Where did I get it?" repeated Laud, evidently startled by the question, so vigorously put. "I told you where I got it."

' Tell me again."

"Captain Shivernock gave it to me."

"What for?"

"I can't tell you that."

"Why not?"

"Because it is a matter between the captain and me."

"I don't care if it is. You said you would answer all my questions, if I would not prosecute."

"Questions about the Maud," explained Laud. "I have told you the secret of my love—"

"Hang the secret of your love!" exclaimed Donald, disgusted with that topic. "I meant all questions."

"But I cannot betray the secrets of Captain Shivernock. My honor—"

"Stick your honor up chimney!" interrupted Donald. "If you go back on the agreement, I shall take the fire before Squire Peters. The question I asked was, why Captain Shivernock gave you four or five hundred dollars?"

"I wish I could answer you, Don John; but I do not feel at liberty to do so just now. I will see the captain, and perhaps I may honorably give you the information you seek."

16

"You needn't mince the matter with me. I know all about it now; but I want it from you."

"All about what?" asked Laud.

"You needn't look green about it. Do you remember the Saturday when I told you the Juno was for sale?"

"I do, very distinctly," answered Laud. "You were in the Juno at the time."

"I was; we parted company, and you stood over towards the Northport shore."

"Just so."

"Over there you met Captain Shivernock."

"I didn't say I did."

"But I say you did," persisted Donald. "For some reason best known to himself, the captain did not want any one to know he was on Long Island that night."

Laud listened with intense interest.

"Do you know what his reason was, Don John?"

"No, I don't. You saw his boat, and overhauled him near the shore."

"Well?"

"You overhauled him near the shore, and he gave you a pile of money not to say that you had seen him."

"It is you who says all this, and not I," added Laud, with more spirit than he had before exhibited. "My honor is not touched."

"I wish you wouldn't say anything more about your honor. It is like a mustard seed in a hay-mow, and I can't see it," snapped Donald.

"You can see that I came honorably by the money."

"Honestly by it; I am satisfied on that point," replied Donald. "If I had not been, I wouldn't have sold you the boat. You see I knew something of Captain Shivernock's movements about that time. If I hadn't, I wouldn't have believed that he gave it to you."

"Then you must have seen the captain at the same time."

"I didn't say I saw him," laughed Donald. "But the wind is breezing up, and we are half way over to Brigadier Island. Come about, Laud."

The skipper acceded to the request, and headed the Juno for Belfast.

CHAPTER XIV.

CAPTAIN SHIVERNOCK'S JOKE.

DONALD considered himself shrewd, sharp, and smart, because he had induced Laud virtually to own that Captain Shivernock had given him the money to purchase his silence, but Donald was not half so shrewd, sharp, and smart as he thought he was.

"Mr. Cavendish, it's no use for us to mince this matter," he continued, determined further to draw out his companion, and feeling happy now, he was very respectful to him.

"Perhaps not, Don John."

"It can do no harm for you and me to talk over this matter. You saw Captain Shivernock on that Saturday morning—didn't you?"

"Of course, if I say I did, you will not let on about it—will you?"

"Not if I can help it; for the fact is, I am in the same boat with you."

"Then you saw the captain."

"Of course I did."

"But what was he doing down there, that made him so particular to keep shady about it?"

"I haven't the least idea. It was the morning after Hasbrook was pounded to a jelly in his own house; but I am satisfied that the captain had nothing to do with it."

"I am not so sure of that," added Laud.

"I am. I went to the captain's house before he returned that day, and both Sykes and his wife told me he had left home at four o'clock that morning, and this was after the pounding was done. Besides, the captain was over on Long Island when I saw him. If he had done the deed, he would have got home before daylight, for the wind was fresh and fair. Instead of that, he was over at Turtle Head when I first saw him. The Juno got aground with him near Seal Harbor, which made him so mad he would not keep her any longer. He was mad because she wasn't a centre-boarder. I suppose after we parted he went over to the Lincolnville or Northport Shore, and hid till after dark in Spruce Harbor, Saturday Cove, or some such place. At any rate, I was at his house in the evening, when he came home."

"The old fellow had been up to some trick, you may depend upon it," added Laud, sagely.

"I came to the conclusion that his desire to keep dark was only a whim, for he is the strangest man that ever walked the earth."

"That's so; but why should he give me such a pile if he hadn't been up to something?"

"And me another pile," added Donald. "We can talk this thing over between ourselves, but not a word to any other person."

"Certainly; I understand. I am paid for holding my tongue, and I intend to do so honorably."

"So do I, until I learn that there is something wrong."

"You have told me some things I did not know before, Don John," suggested Laud.

"You knew that the captain was down by Long Island."

"Yes, but I didn't know he was at Turtle Head; and I am satisfied now that he is the man that shook up Hasbrook that night," continued Laud, in meditative mood.

"Are you? Then I will let the whole thing out," exclaimed Donald.

"No, no! don't do that!" protested Laud. "That wouldn't be fair, at all."

"I would not be a party to the concealment of such an outrage."

"You don't understand it. Hasbrook is a regular swindler."

"That is no reason why he should be pounded half to death in the middle of the night."

"He borrowed a thousand dollars of Captain Shivernock a short time before the outrage. The captain told him he would lend him the money if Hasbrook would give him a good indorser on the paper. After the captain had parted with the money, he ascertained that the indorser was not worth a dollar. Hasbrook had told him the name was that of a rich farmer, and of course the captain was mad. He tried to get back his money, for he knew Hasbrook never paid anything if he could help it. Here is the motive for the outrage," reasoned Laud.

"Why didn't he prosecute him for swindling? for that's what it was."

"Captain Shivernock says he won't trouble any courts to fight his battles for him; he can fight them himself."

"It was wrong to pound any man as Hasbrook was. Why, he wasn't able to go out of the house for a month," added Donald, who was clearly opposed to Lynch law.

Donald was somewhat staggered in his belief by the evidence of his companion, but he determined to inquire further into the matter, and even hoped now that Hasbrook would call upon him.

"One more question, Laud. Do you know where Captain Shivernock got the bills he paid you, and you paid me?" asked he.

"Of course I don't. How should I know where the captain gets his money?" replied Laud, in rather shaky tones.

"True; I didn't much think you would know."

"What odds does it make where he got the bills?" asked Laud, faintly.

"It makes a heap of odds."

"I don't see why."

"I'll tell you why. I paid three of those bills to Mr. Leach to-night for the Maud's suit of sails. One of them was a mended bill."

"Yes, I remember that one, for I noticed it after the captain gave me the money," added Laud.

"Mr. Leach paid that bill to Captain Patterdale."

"To Captain Patterdale!" exclaimed Laud, springing to his feet.

"What odds does it make to you whom he paid it to?" asked Donald, astonished at this sudden demonstration.

"None at all," replied Laud, recovering his self-possession.

"What made you jump so, then?"

"A mosquito bit me," laughed Laud. But it was a graveyard laugh. "Leach paid the bill to Captain Patterdale—you say?"

"Yes, and Captain Patterdale says there is something wrong about the bill," continued Donald, who was far from satisfied with the explanation of his companion.

"What was the matter? Wasn't the bill good?" inquired Laud.

"Yes, the bill was good; but something was wrong, he didn't tell me what."

"That was an odd way to leave it. Why didn't he tell you what was wrong?"

"I don't know. I suppose he knows what he is about, but I don't."

"I should like to know what was wrong about this bill. It has passed through my hands, and it may affect my honor in some way," mused Laud.

"You had better have your honor insured, for

it will get burned up one of these days," added
Donald, as he rose from his seat, and hauled in his
skiff, which was towing astern.

He stepped into the boat, and tossed Laud's
basket to him.

"Here is your basket, Laud," added he. "It
was my evidence against you; and next time, when
you want to burn a yacht, don't leave it on her
deck."

"You will keep shady—won't you, Don John?"
he pleaded.

"That will depend upon what you say and do,"
answered Donald, as he shoved off, and sculled to
the wharf where the Maud lay, to assure himself
that she was in no danger.

He was not quite satisfied to trust her alone all
night, and he decided to sleep in her cabin. He
went to the house, and told Barbara he was afraid
some accident might happen to the yacht, and with
the lantern and some bed-clothes, he returned to
her. He swept up the half-burned shavings, and
threw them overboard. There was not a vestige
of the fire left, and he swabbed up the water with
a sponge. Making his bed on the transom, he lay
down to think over the events of the evening. He

went to sleep after a while, and we will leave him
in this oblivious condition while we follow Laud
Cavendish, who, it cannot be denied, was in a
most unhappy frame of mind. He ran the Juno
up to her moorings, and after he had secured her
sail, and locked up the cabin door, he went on
shore. Undoubtedly he had done an immense
amount of heavy thinking within the last two
hours, and as he was not overstocked with brains,
it wore upon him.

It was nearly ten o'clock in the evening, but
late as it was, Laud walked directly to the house
of Captain Shivernock. There was a light in the
strange man's library, or office, and another in the
dining-room, where the housekeeper usually sat,
which indicated that the family had not retired.
Laud walked up to the side door, and rang the
bell, which was promptly answered by Mrs. Sykes.

"Is Captain Shivernock at home?" asked the
late visitor.

"He is; but he don't see anybody so late as
this," replied the housekeeper.

"I wish to speak to him on very important business, and it is absolutely necessary that I should
see him to-night," persisted Laud.

"I will tell him."

Mrs. Sykes did tell him, and the strange man swore he would not see any one, not even his grandmother, come down from heaven. She reported this answer in substance to Laud.

"I wish to see him on a matter in which he is deeply concerned," said the troubled visitor. "Tell him, if you please, in regard to the Hasbrook affair."

Perhaps Mrs. Sykes knew something about the Hasbrook affair herself, for she promptly consented to make this second application for the admission of the stranger, for such he was to her.

She returned in a few moments with an invitation to enter, and so it appeared that there was some power in the "Hasbrook affair." Laud was conducted to the library,—as the retired shipmaster chose to call the apartment, though there were not a dozen books in it,—where the captain sat in a large rocking-chair, with his feet on the table.

"Who are you?" demanded the strange man; and we are obliged to modify his phraseology in order to make it admissible to our pages.

"Mr. Laud Cavendish, at your service," replied he, politely.

"*Mister* Laud Cavendish!" repeated the captain, with a palpable sneer; "you are the swell that used to drive the grocery wagon."

"I was formerly employed at Miller's store, but I am not there now."

"Well, what do you want here?"

"I wish to see you, sir."

"You do see me—don't you?" growled the eccentric. "What's your business?"

"On the morning after the Hasbrook outrage, Captain Shivernock, you were seen at Seal Harbor," said Laud.

"Who says I was?" roared the captain, springing to his feet.

"I beg your pardon sir; but I say so," answered Laud, apparently unmoved by the violence of his auditor. "You were in the boat formerly owned by Mr. Ramsay, and you ran over towards the Northport shore."

"Did you see me?"

"I did," replied Laud.

"And you have come to levy black-mail upon me," added the captain, with a withering stare at his visitor.

"Nothing of the sort, sir. I claim to be a gentleman."

"O, you do!"

Captain Shivernock laughed heartily.

"I do, sir. I am not capable of anything derogatory to the character of a gentleman."

"Bugs and brickbats!" roared the strange man, with another outburst of laughter. "You are a gentleman! That's good! And you won't do anything derogatory to the character of a gentleman. That's good, too!"

"I trust I have the instincts of a gentleman," added Laud, smoothing down his jet mustache.

"I trust you have; but what do you want of me, if you have the instincts of a gentleman, and don't bleed men with money when you think you have them on the hip?"

"If you will honor me with your attention a few moments, I will inform you what I want of you."

"Good again!" chuckled the captain. "I will honor you with my attention. You have got cheek enough to fit out a life insurance agency."

"I am not the only one who saw you that Saturday morning," said Laud.

"Who else saw me?"

"Don John."

"How do you know he did?"

"He told me so."

"The young hypocrite!" exclaimed the strange man, with an oath. "I made it a rule years ago never to trust a man or a boy who has much to do with churches and Sunday Schools. The little snivelling puppy! And he has gone back on me."

"It is only necessary for me to state facts," answered Laud. "You can form your own conclusions, without any help from me."

"Perhaps I can," added Captain Shivernock, who seemed to be in an unusual humor on this occasion, for the pretentious manners of his visitor appeared to amuse rather than irritate him.

"Again, sir, Jacob Hasbrook, of Lincolnville, believes you are the man who pounded him to a jelly that night," continued Laud.

"Does he?" laughed the captain. "Well, that is a good joke; but I want to say that I respect the man who did it, whoever he is."

"Self-respect is a gentlemanly quality. The man who don't respect himself will not be respected by others," said Laud, stroking his chin.

"Eh?"

Laud confidently repeated the proposition.

"You respect yourself, and of course you respect the man that pounded Hasbrook," he added.

"Do you mean to say I flogged Hasbrook?" demanded the strange man, doubling his fist, and shaking it savagely in Laud's face.

"It isn't for me to say that you did, for you know better than I do; but you will pardon me if I say that the evidence points in this direction. Hasbrook has been over to Belfast several times to work up his case. The last time I saw him he was looking for Don John, who, I am afraid, is rather leaky."

In spite of his bluff manners, Laud saw that the captain was not a little startled by the information just imparted.

"The miserable little psalm-singer," growled the strange man, walking the room, muttering to himself. "If he disobeys my orders, I'll thrash him worse than—Hasbrook was thrashed."

"It is unpleasant to be suspected of a crime, and revolting to the instincts of a gentleman," added Laud.

"Do you mean to say that I am suspected of a crime, you long-eared puppy?" yelled the captain.

"I beg your pardon, Captain Shivernock, but it

isn't agreeable to a gentleman to be called by such opprobrious names," said Laud, rising from his chair, and taking his round-top hat from the table. "I am willing to leave you, but not to be insulted."

Laud looked like the very impersonation of dignity itself, as he walked towards the door.

"Stop!" yelled the captain.

"I do not know that any one but Hasbrook suspects you of a crime," Laud explained.

"I'm glad he does suspect me," added the strange man, more gently. "Whoever did that job served him just right, and I envy the man that did it."

"Still, it is unpleasant to be suspected of a crime."

"It wasn't a crime."

"People call it so; but I sympathize with you, for like you I am suspected of a crime, of which, like yourself, I am innocent."

"Are you, indeed? And what may your crime be, Mr. Cavendish?"

"It is in this connection that I wish to state my particular business with you."

17

"Go on and state it, and don't be all night about it."

"I may add that I also came to warn you against the movements of Hasbrook. I will begin at the beginning."

"Begin, then; and don't go round Cape Horn in doing it," snarled the captain.

"I will, sir. Captain Patterdale—"

"Another miserable psalm-singer. Is he in the scrape?"

"He is, sir. He has lost a tin box, which contained nearly fourteen hundred dollars in cash, besides many valuable papers."

"I'm glad of it; and I hope he never will find it," was the kindly expression of the eccentric nabob for the Christian nabob. "Was the box lost or stolen?"

"Stolen, sir."

"So much the better. I hope the thief will never be discovered."

Laud did not say how he happpened to know that the tin box had been stolen, for Captain Patterdale, the deputy sheriff, and Nellie were supposed to be the only persons who had any knowledge of the fact.

"It appears that in this tin box there was a certain fifty-dollar bill, which had been torn into four parts, and mended by pasting two strips of paper upon it, one extending from right to left, and the other from top to bottom, on the back."

"Eh?" interposed the wicked nabob. "Wait a minute."

The captain opened an iron safe in the room, and from a drawer took out a handful of bank bills. From these he selected three, and tossed them on the table.

"Like those?" he inquired, with interest.

"Exactly like them," replied Laud, astonished to find that each was the counterpart of the one he had paid Donald for the Juno, and had the "white cross of Denmark" upon it.

"Do you know how those bills happened to be in that condition, Mr. Cavendish?" chuckled the captain.

"Of course I do not, sir."

"I'll tell you, my gay buffer. I have got a weak, soft place somewhere in my gizzard; 1 don't know where; if I did, I'd cut it out. About three months ago, just after I brought from Portland one hundred of these new fifty-dollar bills, there was a great cry here for money for some missionary concern. I read something in the newspaper, at this time, about what some of the missionaries had done for a lot of sailors who had been cast away on the South Sea Islands. I thought more of the psalm-singers than ever before, and I was tempted to do something for them. Well, I actually wrote to some parson here who was howling for money, and stuck four of those bills between the leaves. I think it is very likely I should have sent them to the parson, if I hadn't been called out of the room. I threw the note, with the bills in it, on the table, and went out to see a pair of horses a jockey had driven into the yard for me to look at. When I came back and glanced at the note, I thought what a fool I had been, to think of giving money to those canting psalm-singers. I was mad with myself for my folly, and I tore the note into four pieces before I thought that the bills were in it. But Mrs. Sykes mended them as you see. Go on with your yarn, my buffer.''

"That bill I paid to Don John for the Juno," continued Laud. "He paid it to Mr. Leach, the sail-maker, who paid it to Captain Patterdale, and he says it was one of the bills in the tin chest when it was stolen. Don John says he had it from me."

"Precisely so; and that is what makes it unpleasant to be suspected of a crime," laughed Captain Shivernock. "But you don't state where you got the bill, Mr. Cavendish. Perhaps you don't wish to tell."

"I shall tell the whole story with the greatest pleasure," added Laud. "I was sailing one day down by Haddock Ledge, when I saw a man tumble overboard from a boat moored where he had been fishing. He was staving drunk, and went forward, as I thought, to get up his anchor. The boat rolled in the sea, and over he went. I got him out. The cold water sobered him in a measure, and he was very grateful to me. He went to his coat, which he did not wear when he fell, and took from his pocket a roll of bills. He counted off ten fifties, and gave them to me. Feeling sure that I had saved his life, I did not think five hundred dollars was any too much to pay for it, and I took the money. I don't think he would have given me so much if he hadn't been drunk. I asked him who he was, but he would not tell me, saying he didn't want his friends in Boston to know he had been over the bay, and in the bay; but he said he had been staying in Belfast a couple of days.''

"Good story!'' laughed the wicked nabob.

"Every word of it is as true as preaching,'' protested Laud.

"Just about,'' added the captain, who hadn't much confidence in preaching.

"You can see, Captain Shivernock, that I am in an awkward position,'' added Laud. "I have no doubt the man I saved was the one who stole the tin box. He paid me with the stolen bills.''

"It is awkward, as you say,'' chuckled the strange man. "I suppose you wouldn't know the fellow you saved if you saw him.''

"O, yes, I think I should,'' exclaimed Laud. "But suppose, when Captain Patterdale comes to me to inquire where I got the marked bill, I should tell him this story. He wouldn't believe a word of it.''

"He would be a fool if he did,'' exclaimed Captain Shivernock, with a coarse grin. "Therefore, my gay buffer, don't tell it to him.''

"But I must tell him where I got the bill," pleaded Laud.

"Ha, ha, ha!" laughed the eccentric, shaking his sides as though they were agitated by a young earthquake. "Tell him I gave you the bill!"

The captain seemed to be intensely amused at the novel idea; and Laud did not object; on the contrary, he seemed to appreciate the joke. It was midnight when he left the house, and went to the Juno to sleep in her cabin. If he had gone home earlier in the evening, he might have seen Captain Patterdale, who did him the honor to make a late call upon him.

CHAPTER XV.

LAUD CAVENDISH TAKES CARE OF HIMSELF.

DONALD did not sleep very well in the cabin of the Maud, not only because his bed was very hard and uncomfortable, but because he was troubled; and before morning he fully realized the truth of the saying, in regard to certain persons, that "they choose darkness, because their deeds are evil." He wished he had not consented to keep the secret of either Captain Shivernock or Laud Cavendish, and was afraid he had compromised hsmself by his silence. When he turned out in the morning, he believed he had hardly slept a wink all night, though he had actually slumbered over six hours; but a person who lies awake in the darkness, especially if his thoughts are troublesome, lengthens minutes into hours. But Donald welcomed the morning light when he awoke, and the bright sun which streamed through the trunk ports. He went to the shop, and for two hours before his men arrived worked on the tender of the Maud.

The mast of the yacht was stepped during the forenoon, and after dinner the rigger came to do his part of the work. Samuel Rodman was now so much interested in the progress of the labor on the new yacht, that he spent nearly all his time on board of her. The top mast, gaff, and boom were all ready to go into their places, and the Maud looked as though she was nearly completed. All the members of the Yacht Club were impatient for her to be finished, for the next regatta had been postponed a week, so that the Maud could take part in the affair; and the club were to go on a cruise for ten days, after the race.

There was no little excitement in the club in relation to the Maud. Donald had confidently asserted his belief, weeks before, that she would outsail the Skylark, not as a mere boast, but as a matter of business. His father had made an improvement upon the model of the Sea Foam, which he was reasonably certain would give her the advantage. The young boat-builder had also remedied a slight defect in the arrangement of the centre-board in the Maud, had added a little to the size of the jib and mainsail, and he hoped these alterations would tell in favor of the new craft, while they would not take anything from her stiffness in heavy weather.

"I believe the old folks are as much interested in the next race as the members of the club, Don John," said Rodman, one day, as he came upon the wharf.

"I am glad they are," replied Donald, laughing. "It will make business good for Ramsay & Son."

"Half a dozen of them are going to make up a first prize of one hundred dollars for the regatta; so that the winner of the race will make a good thing by it," added Rodman.

"That will be a handsome prize."

"If the Maud takes it, Don John, the money shall be yours, as you are to sail her."

"O, no!" exclaimed Donald. "I don't believe in that. The prize will belong to the boat."

"If you win the race in the Maud, I shall be satisfied with the glory, without any of the spoils."

"Well, we won't quarrel about it now, for she may not win the first prize."

"Well, the same gentlemen will give a second

prize of fifty dollars," continued Rodman. "But don't you expect to get the first prize, Don John?"

"I do; but to expect is not always to win, you know."

"You have always talked as though you felt pretty sure of coming in first," said Rodman, who did not like to see any abatement of confidence on the part of the boat-builder.

"It is the easiest thing in the world to be mistaken, Sam. If the Maud loses the first prize, I may as well shut up shop, and take a situation in a grocery store, for my business would be ruined."

"Not quite so bad as that, I hope," added Rodman.

"Mr. Norwood is waiting to see how she sails, before he orders a yacht for Frank. Can't you invite Frank and his father to sail with us in the race?"

"Certainly, if you desire it, Don John," replied Rodman. "Mr. Norwood is a big man, and he will be a capital live weight for us, if it happens to blow fresh."

"I hope it will blow; if it don't, the Christabel is sure of the first prize. I want just such a day as we had when the Sea Foam cleaned out the Skylark."

"That was a little too much of a good thing. You came pretty near taking the mast out of the Sea Foam that day."

"Not at all; our masts don't come out so easily as that, though I think the mast of the Sea Foam would snap before she would capsize."

"I like that in a boat; it is a good thing to have a craft that will stay right side up. The fellows have got another idea, Don John."

"Well, ideas are good things to have. What is it now?" asked Donald.

"They are going to build a club-house over on Turtle Head."

"On Turtle Head! Why don't they have it down on Manhegan?" which is an island ten miles from the coast of Maine.

"It will be only a shanty, where the fellows can have a good time, and get up chowders. They talk of hiring a hall in the city, and having meetings for mutual improvement during the fall and winter."

"That will be a capital idea."

"We can have a library of books on nautical and other subjects, take the newspapers and magazines, and hang up pictures of yachts and other vessels on the walls. I hope, when you get the Maud done, you will not be so busy, Don John, for you don't attend many of our club meetings.''

''I hope to be busier than ever. You see, Sam, I can't afford to run with you rich fellows. I don't wear kid gloves,'' laughed Donald.

''No matter if you don't; you are just as good a fellow as any of them.''

''Everybody uses me first rate; as well as though my father had been a nabob.''

''Well, they ought to; for it is brains, not money, that makes the man. We want to see more of you in the club. You must go with us on our long cruise.''

''I am afraid I can't spare the time. Ten days is a good while; but it will depend upon whether I get the job to build Mr. Norwood's yacht.''

Donald would gladly have spent more time with the club, but his conscience would not permit him to neglect his business. He felt that his success depended entirely upon his own industry and diligence; and he never left his work, except when the occasion fully justified him in doing so. He attended all the regattas as a matter of business, as well as of pleasure; and he had seen the Sea

Foam beaten twice by the Skylark since he won the memorable race in the former. Edward Patterdale was fully satisfied, now, that a skilful boatman was as necessary as a fast boat, in order to win the honors of the club, and he wished Donald to "coach" him, until he obtained the skill to compete with the commodore. Donald had promised to do it, as soon as he had time, and the owner of the Sea Foam hoped the opportunity would be afforded during the long cruise.

The work on the Maud was hurried forward as rapidly as was consistent with thoroughness, and in a few days she was ready for the last coats of paint. The boat-builder was favored with good, dry weather, and on the day before the great regatta, she was ready to receive her furniture and stores. The paint was dry and hard; but when the stove-dealer came with the little galley for the cook-room, the deck was carefully covered with old cloths, the cushions were placed on the transoms, the oil-cloth carpet was laid on the floor by Kennedy, who was experienced in this kind of work, and Samuel Rodman was as busy as a bee arranging the crockery ware and stores which he had purchased. It only remained to bend on the sails, which was accomplished early in the afternoon.

With Mr. Rodman, Samuel, and the two workmen on board, Donald made a trial trip in the new craft. The party went down the bay as far as Seal Harbor; but the wind was rather light for her, and she had no opportunity to show her sailing qualities, though with her gaff-topsail and the balloon-jib, she walked by everything afloat that day.

"I am entirely satisfied with her, Don John," said Mr. Rodman, as the Maud approached the city on her return. "I think she will sail well."

"I hope she will, sir," replied Donald. "To-morrow will prove what there is in her."

"She is well built and handsomely finished, and whether she wins the race or not I shall be satisfied. I never looked upon a handsomer yacht in my life. You have done your work admirably, Don John."

"Mr. Kennedy did the joiner work," said Donald, willing to have his foreman, as he called him, share the honors of the day.

"He did it well."

"I only did just what my boss ordered me to

do," laughed Kennedy; "and I want to say, that I didn't do the first thing towards planning any part of her. Don John hasn't often asked for any advice from me. He is entitled to all the credit."

"I have no doubt you did all you could to make the job a success," added Mr. Rodman.

"I did; and so did Walker," said Kennedy, indicating the other ship carpenter. "Both of us did our very best, never idling a moment, or making a bad joint; and I can say, there isn't a better built craft in the United States than this yacht. Not a knot or a speck of rot has been put into her. Everything has been done upon honor, and she will be stiff enough to cross the Atlantic in midwinter. I'd rather be in her than in many a ship I've worked on."

"I'm glad to know all this," replied Mr. Rodman. "Now, Don John, if the firm of Ramsay & Son is ready to deliver the Maud, I will give you a check for the balance due on her."

Donald was all ready, and after the yacht had been moored off the wharf where she had been completed, the business was transacted in the shop. A bill of sale was given, and the boatbuilder received a check for four hundred dollars, which he carried into the house and showed to his mother. Of course the good lady was delighted with the success of her son, and Barbara laughed till she shook her curls into a fearful snarl.

"You have done well, Donald," said Mrs. Ramsay. "I thank God that you have been so successful."

"I have paid nearly all my bills, and I shall make about two hundred and fifty dollars on the job," added the young boat-builder. "I think I can build the next one for less money."

"You may not get another one to build, my son."

"That depends upon the race to-morrow. If I beat the Skylark, I'm sure of one."

"Don't be too confident."

"I am to sail the Maud to-morrow, and if there is any speed in her, as I think there is, I shall get it out of her. To-morrow will be a big day for me; but if I lose the race, the firm of Ramsay & Son is used up."

Donald put the check in his wallet, and went out to the shop again, where he found Samuel Rodman looking for him. The owner of the Maud was so delighted with the craft, that he could not

18

keep away from her, and he wanted to go on board again.

"Bob Montague is going to give you a hard pull to-morrow, Don John," said Rodman, as they got into the tender.   .

"I hope he will do his best; and the harder the pull, the better," replied Donald.

"If we only beat him," suggested Rodman.

"I expect to beat him; but I may be mistaken."

"Bob hauled up the Skylark on the beach this afternoon, and rubbed her bottom with black lead."

"I am glad to hear it."

"Glad? Why?"

"It proves that he means business."

"Of course he means business."

"'I wonder if he knows I am to build a yacht for Mr. Norwood, in case I win this race."

"I don't believe he does. I never heard of it till you told me."

"He is such a splendid fellow, that I was afraid he would *let* me beat him, if he knew I was to make anything by it."

"I think it very likely he would."

"But I want to beat the Skylark fairly, or not at all."

"There comes Laud Cavendish," said Rodman, as the Juno came up the bay, and bore down upon the Maud. "He was blackballed in the club the other day, and he don't feel good. Let's go ashore again, and wait till he sheers off, for I don't want to see him. He will be sure to go on board of the yacht if we are there, for he is always poking his nose in where he is not wanted."

Donald, who was at the oars, pulled back to the shore. The Juno ran close up to the Maud, tacked, and stood up the bay.

"He is gone," said Rodman. "I don't want him asking me why he was blackballed. He is an intolerable spoony."

"Don John!" called some one, as he was shoving off the tender.

Donald looked up, and saw Mr. Beardsley, the deputy sheriff, who had been working up the tin box case with Captain Patterdale.

"I want to see you," added the officer.

Donald wondered if Mr. Beardsley wanted to see him officially; but he was thankful that he was able to look even a deputy sheriff square in the face.

He jumped out of the tender, and Rodman went off to the yacht alone. We are somewhat better informed than the young boat-builder in regard to the visit of the sheriff, and we happen to know that he did come officially; and in order to explain why it was so, it is necessary to go back to the point where we left Mr. Laud Cavendish. He slept in the cabin of the Juno after he left the house of Captain Shivernock. He did not sleep any better than Donald Ramsay that night; and the long surges rolled in by the paddle-wheels of the steamer Richmond, as she came into the harbor early the next morning, awoke him.

The first thing he thought of was his visit to the house of the strange man; the next was his breakfast, and he decided to go on shore, and get the meal at a restaurant. The Juno was moored near the steamboat wharf, where the Portland boat made her landings. This was a convenient place for him to disembark, and he pulled in his tender to the pier. As he approached the landing steps, he saw Captain Shivernock hastening down the wharf with a valise in his hand. It was evident that he was going up the river, perhaps to Bangor. Laud did not like the idea of the captain's going away just at that time. Donald had told Captain Patterdale that the mended bill came from him, and of course the owner of the tin box would immediately come to him for further information.

"Then, if I tell him Captain Shivernock gave it to me, he will want to see him; and he won't be here to be seen," reasoned Laud. "I can't explain why the captain gave me the money, and in his absence I shall be in a bad fix. I must take care of myself."

Laud went to the restaurant, and ate his breakfast; after which he returned to the Juno. He took care of himself by getting under way, and standing over towards Castine, where he dined that day. Then he continued his voyage down the bay, through Edgemoggin Reach to Mount Desert, where he staid several days, living upon "the fat of the land" and the fish of the sea, which go well together. When he was confident that Captain Shivernock had returned, he sailed for Belfast, and arrived after a two days' voyage. The strange man had not come back, and Laud thought it very singular that he had not. Then he began to wonder why the captain had laughed so unreasonably long and loud when he told him to say that he had given him the mended bill. Laud could not see the joke at the time; but now he concluded that the laugh came in because he was going away on a long journey, and would not be in town to answer any questions which Captain Patterdale might propose.

Mr. Cavendish was disturbed, and felt that he was a victim of a practical joke, and he determined to get out of the way again. Unfortunately for him, he had shown himself in the city, and before he could leave he was interviewed by Captain Patterdale and Mr. Beardsley. The white cross of Denmark was pleasantly alluded to again by the former, and exhibited to Laud. Did he know that bill? Had he ever seen it before?

He did not know it; had never seen it.

It was no use to say, in the absence of that gentleman, that Captain Shivernock had given him the bill. It would be equally foolish to tell the Haddock Ledge story in the absence of the generous stranger, who had declined to give his name, though he was kind enough to say that he had spent a few days in Belfast. Since neither of these fictions was available in the present emergency, Laud "went back" on Donald Ramsay. He did not love the boat-builder, and so it was not a sacrifice of personal feeling for him to do it. On

the contrary, he would rather like to get his
"rival," as he chose to regard him, out of the
way.

"But you paid him a considerable sum of money
some two months ago," suggested Captain Patterdale.

"Not a red!" protested Laud. "I never paid
him any money in my life."

"You bought the Juno of him."

"No, sir; nor of any one else. She don't belong to me."

"But you are using her all the time."

"Captain Shivernock got tired of her, and lets
me have the use of her for taking care of her."

"Didn't you say you owned her, and that you
were going to change her name from Juno to Nellie?" demanded the captain, sternly.

"I did; but that was all gas," replied Laud,
with a sickly grin.

"If you would lie about one thing, perhaps you
would about another," said the captain.

"I was only joking when I said I owned the
Juno. If you will go up to Captain Shivernock's
house, he will tell you all about it."

That was a plain way to solve the problem, and

they went to the strange man's house. Laud knew the captain was not at home; but his persecutors gave him the credit of suggesting this step. Sykes and his wife were at home. They did not know whether or not Captain Shivernock had given Laud the use of the Juno, but presumed he had, for the young man was in the house with him half the night, about ten days before. Thus far everything looked well for Laud; and the Sykeses partially confirmed his statements.

"Now, Captain Patterdale, I have answered all your questions, and I wish you would answer mine. What's the matter?" said Laud, putting on his boldest face.

"Never mind what the matter is."

"Well, I know as well as you do. I used to think Don John was a good fellow, and liked him first rate. I didn't think he would be mean enough to shove his own guilt upon me," replied Laud.

"What do you mean by that?" demanded Captain Patterdale.

"Though I knew about it all the time, I didn't mean to say a word."

"About what?"

The Papers from the Tin Box.   Page 281

"About your tin trunk. We didn't keep any such in our store! I knew what you meant all the time; but I didn't let on that Don John had done it."

"Done what?"

"Stolen it. That day I was in the library with Don John and Hasbrook, I was discharged from Miller's, because I wanted to go away to stay over Sunday. I had a boat down by Ramsay's shop, and I went there to get off. Well, captain, I saw Don John have the same tin trunk I saw in your library."

"Are you telling the truth?"

"Of course I am. I wouldn't go back on Don John if he hadn't tried to lay it to me. If you search his house and shop, I'll bet you'll find the tin trunk, or some of the money and papers."

Captain Patterdale was intensely grieved, even to believe Laud's statement was possibly true; but he decided to have the boat-builder's premises searched before he proceeded any further against Laud. Mr. Beardsley was to do this unpleasant duty, and for this purpose he called on Donald the night before the great race.

The deputy sheriff did his work thoroughly, in

spite of the confidence of Donald and the distress of his mother and sister. Perhaps he would not have discovered the four fifty-dollar bills concealed in the bureau if Donald had not assisted him; but he had no help in finding a lot of notes and other papers hidden under a sill in the shop. The boat-builder protested that he knew nothing about these papers, and had never seen them before in his life.

Mrs. Ramsay and Barbara wept as though their hearts would break; but Donald was led away by the sheriff.

That night Captain Shivernock returned by the train from Portland.

CHAPTER XVI.

SATURDAY COVE.

MR. BEARDSLEY, the deputy sheriff, conducted Donald to the elegant mansion of Captain Patterdale. Perhaps no one who saw them walking together suspected that the boat-builder was charged with so gross a crime as stealing the tin box and its valuable contents. Some persons do not like to walk through the streets with sheriffs and policemen; but Donald was not of that sort, for in spite of all the evidence brought against him, he obstinately refused to believe that he was guilty. Even the fact that several notes and other papers had been found in the shop did not impair his belief in his own innocence. Captain Patterdale was in his library nervously awaiting the return of the officer, when they arrived.

"Don John, I hope you will come out of this all right," said he, as they entered.

"I have no doubt I shall, sir," replied Donald. "If I don't, it will be because I can't prove what is the truth."

Mr. Beardsley reported the result of the search, and handed the captain the four fifty-dollar bills with the papers.

"I have no doubt all these were in the tin box," said the nabob, sadly. "The bills are like those paid me by Hasbrook, and these notes are certainly mine. I don't ask you to commit yourself, Don John, but—"

"Commit myself!" exclaimed Donald, with a look of contempt, which, in this connection, was sublime. "I mean to speak the truth, whether I am committed or not."

"Perhaps you will be able to clear this thing up," added Captain Patterdale. "I wish to ask you a few questions."

"I will answer them truly. The only wrong I have done was to conceal what I thought there was no harm in concealing."

"It is not wise to do things in the dark."

"You will excuse me, sir, but you have done the same thing. If I had known that your tin box was stolen, I should have understood several things which are plain to me now."

"What, for instance?"

"If I had known it, I should have brought these bills to you as soon as Laud paid them to me, to see if they belonged to you. And I should have known why Laud was digging clams on Turtle Head."

"Laud says he paid you no money."

"He paid me three hundred and fifty dollars for the Juno—these four bills and the three I paid Mr. Leach."

"He persists that he don't own the Juno, and says that Captain Shivernock lets him have the use of her for taking care of her," continued the nabob.

Donald's face, which had thus far been clouded with anxiety, suddenly lighted up with a cheerful smile, as he produced the cover of an old tuck-diary, which contained the papers of Ramsay & Son. He opened it, and took therefrom the bill of sale of the Juno, in the well-known writing of Captain Shivernock.

"Does that prove anything?" he asked, as he tossed the paper on the desk, within reach of the inquisitor.

"It proves that Captain Shivernock sold the Juno to you, and consequently he has not owned her since the date of this bill," replied the nabob, as he read the paper.

"Is it likely, then, that Captain Shivernock lets Laud have the use of her for taking care of her?" demanded Donald, warmly.

"Certainly not."

"Is it any more likely that, if I own the Juno, I should let Laud use her for nothing, for he says he never paid me a dollar?"

"I don't think it is."

"Then you can believe as much as you please of the rest of Laud's story, which Mr. Beardsley related to me as we walked up," added Donald.

"He says he saw you have the tin box, Don John."

"And I saw him digging clams in the loam on Turtle Head."

"What do you mean by that?"

"I think he buried the tin box there. I saw where he had been digging, but I didn't know any tin box had been stolen then, and thought nothing of it," answered Donald.

At this moment there was a tremendous ring at

the door bell, a ring that evidently "meant business." Captain Patterdale opened the door himself, and Captain Shivernock stalked into the room
as haughtily as though he owned the elegant mansion. He had been to Newport and Cape May to
keep cool, and had arrived a couple of hours before
from Portland. Mrs. Sykes had told him all the
news she could in this time, and among other
things informed him that Captain Patterdale and
the deputy sheriff had called to inquire whether
Laud had the use of the boat for taking care of
her. By this he knew that the tin trunk matter
was under investigation. He was interested, and
possibly he was alarmed; at any rate, he went to
his safe, put the roll of fifty-dollar bills in his
pocket, and hastened over to Captain Patterdale's
house.

"When people come to my house, and I'm not
at home, I don't like to have them talk to my ser-
vants about my affairs," blustered the strange
man.

"I don't think we meddled with your affairs
any further than to ask if Laud Cavendish had the
use of the Juno for taking care of her," explained
Captain Patterdale.

"It don't concern you. Laud Cavendish does have the use of the Juno for taking care of her."

"Indeed!" exclaimed the good nabob, glancing at Donald.

"Indeed!" sneered the wicked nabob. "You needn't *indeed* anything I say. I can speak the truth better than you psalm-singers."

"I am very glad you can, Captain Shivernock, for that is what we are in need of just now," laughed the good nabob. "And since we have meddled with your affairs in your absence, it is no more than right that we should explain the reason for doing so. A tin box, containing nearly fourteen hundred dollars in bills, and many valuable papers, was stolen from this room. Three persons, Jacob Hasbrook, Laud Cavendish, and Don John here, passed through the library when they left the house."

"Hasbrook stole it; he is the biggest scoundrel of the three," added the wicked nabob.

"Perhaps not," continued the good nabob. "A bill which I can identify came back to me the other day. Don John paid it to Mr. Leach, and he to me. Don John says Laud Cavendish paid him the bill."

"And so he did," protested Donald, as the captain glanced at him.

"And I gave it to Laud Cavendish," added Captain Shivernock; thus carrying out the programme which had been agreed upon the night before he went on his journey.

Possibly, if Mr. Laud Cavendish had known that the wicked nabob had returned, he would have hastened to see him, and inform him of the change he had made in the programme. If he had done so, their stories might have agreed better. Captain Patterdale, Mr. Beardsley, and Donald were astonished at this admission.

"For what did you pay it to him?" asked the good nabob.

"None of your business what I paid it to him for. That's my affair," bluffed the wicked nabob.

"But this bill was in the box."

"But how do you know it was? I suppose you will say next that I stole the box."

"I hope you will assist me in tracing out this matter," said the good nabob, as he produced the mended bill. "This is the one; I call it the white cross of Denmark."

19

Captain Shivernock picked up the bill, and took from his pocket his own roll of fifties.

"You must admit that the bill is peculiar enough to be easily identified," added Captain Patterdale.

"I don't admit it," said the strange man, as he threw the four mended bills together on the desk.

"Now, which is it?"

The wicked nabob laughed and roared in his delight when he saw the confusion of the good nabob.

"They are very like," said the good.

"But three of them are mine, and haven't been out of my hands since the 'white cross of Denmark' was put upon them," added the wicked, still shaking his sides with mirth.

"Still I can indentify the one that was in the box. That is it;" and Captain Patterdale held up the right one. "This has been folded, while yours have simply been rolled, and have not a crease in them. Hasbrook paid me the money that was stolen."

"The villain swindled it out of me," growled the wicked.

"But he folded his money, however he got it," continued the good.

"I can bring you a dozen bills with the white cross on them," blustered the wicked, "and all of them folded like that one."

"Can you tell where you got it, captain?"

"From the bank," replied he, promptly; and then more to have his hit at the missionaries than to explain the white cross, he told how the bills were torn. "That's all I have to say," he added; and he stalked out of the house, in spite of the host's request for him to remain, without giving a word or even a look to Donald.

"I am astonished," said Captain Patterdale. "Can it be possible that he paid that bill to Laud?"

Perhaps this was the joke of the strange man— simply to confuse and confound a "psalm-singer."

"It looks as though we had lost the clew," said the deputy sheriff. "At any rate, Don John's story is confirmed."

"Why should the captain give Laud so much money?" mused the nabob.

"I know," said Donald. "I told you, in the first place, that I knew where Laud got the money to pay for the Juno; but it was a great secret affecting another person, and he wished me not to tell."

"I remember that, Don John," added the captain.

"He told me that Captain Shivernock gave him the money; but he would not tell me why he gave it to him; but I knew without any telling, for the captain gave me sixty dollars, besides the Juno, for holding my tongue."

"About what?" asked the nabob, deeply interested in the narrative.

"I don't understand the matter myself; but I will state all the facts, though Captain Shivernock threatened to kill me if I did so. On the morning after the Hasbrook outrage, while I was waiting on Turtle Head for the Yacht Club to arrive, the captain came to the Head, saying he had walked over from Seal Harbor, where he had got aground in his boat. I sailed him down, and on the way he gave me the money. Then he said I was not to mention the fact that I had seen him on Long Island, or anywhere else. I didn't make any promises, and told him I wouldn't lie about it. Then he gave me the Juno, and took my boat, which he returned that night. After I went up in the Juno, I met Laud, and offered to sell him the boat. When we parted, he stood over towards the Northport shore, where Captain Shivernock had gone, and I thought they would meet; but I lost sight of them.''

''Then you think the captain paid Laud the money when they met.''

''That was what I supposed when Laud paid me for the boat. I believed it was all right. I had a talk with Laud afterwards about it, and I told him how he got the money. He did not deny what I said.''

''This was the morning after the Hasbrook outrage—was it?'' asked Mr. Beardsley.

''Yes, it was; but I knew nothing about that till night.''

''We can easily understand why the captain did not want to be seen near Lincolnville,'' added the sheriff. ''It was he who pounded Hasbrook for swindling him.''

''No, sir; I think not,'' interposed Donald. ''I inquired into that matter myself. Mr. Sykes and his wife both told me, before the captain got home, that he left his house at four o'clock in the morning.''

"I am afraid they were instructed to say that," said the nabob.

"They shall have a chance to say it in court under oath," added the officer; "for I will arrest the captain to-morrow for the outrage. I traced the steps of a man over to Saturday Cove, in Northport, and that is where he landed."

"Was it the print of the captain's boot?" asked the nabob.

"No; but I have a theory which I shall work up to-morrow. Don John's evidence is the first I have obtained, that amounts to anything."

"If he pounded Hasbrook, why should he run over to Seal Harbor, when he had a fair wind to come up?" asked Donald.

"To deceive you, as it seems he has," laughed Mr. Beardsley. "Probably getting aground deranged his plans."

"But he ran over to Northport after we parted."

"Because it was a better place to conceal himself during the day. Sykes says he went down to Vinal Haven that day. I know he did not. Now, Don John, we must go to Turtle Head to-night, and see about that box."

"I am ready, sir."

"I will go with you," added Captain Patterdale; "and we will take the Sea Foam."

Donald was permitted to go home and comfort his mother with the assurance that he was entirely innocent of the crime with which he was charged; and great was the joy of his mother and sister. The mainsail of the Sea Foam was hoisted when he went on board. The wind was rather light, and it was midnight before the yacht anchored off Turtle Head. The party went ashore in the tender, the sheriff carrying a lantern and a shovel. Donald readily found the place where the earth had been disturbed by Laud's clam-digger. Mr. Beardsley dug till he came to a rock, and it was plain that no tin box was there.

"But I am sure that Laud had been digging here, for I saw the print of his clam-digger," said Donald.

"This hole had been dug before," added the sheriff.

"Even Laud Cavendish would not be fool enough to bury the box in such an exposed place as this," suggested Captain Patterdale.

"I know he came down here on the day the box was stolen," said Donald, "and that he was here with his clam-digger on the day I met Captain Shivernock. He must have put those papers in the shop."

"If the box was ever buried here, it has been removed," added the captain.

"Just look at the dirt which came out of the hole," continued Mr. Beardsley, pointing to the heap, and holding the lantern over it. "What I threw out last is beach gravel. That was put in to fill up the hole after he had taken out the box. When he first buried it, he had to carry off some of the yellow loam. In my opinion, the box has been here."

"It is not here now, and we may as well return," replied Captain Patterdale. 'I am really more desirous of finding the papers in the box than the money."

"He has only chosen a new hiding-place for it," said the sheriff. "If we say nothing, and keep an eye on him for a few days, we may find it."

As this was all that could be done, the party returned to the city; and early in the morning Donald went to bed, to obtain the rest he needed before the great day. Possibly Mr. Beardsley

More Evidence.   Page 299.

slept some that night, though it is certain he was at Saturday Cove, in Northport, the next forenoon. He had a "theory;" and when a man has a theory, he will sometimes go without his sleep in order to prove its truth or its falsity. Jacob Hasbrook was with him, and quite as much interested in the theory as the officer, who desired to vindicate his reputation as a detective. He had driven to the house of the victim of the outrage, and looked the matter over again in the light of the evidence obtained from the boat-builder.

"I have been trying to see Donald Ramsay," said Hasbrook. "I have been to his shop four times, but he's always off on some boat scrape. You say he saw Captain Shivernock the next morning."

"Yes; and the captain didn't want to be seen, which is the best part of the testimony. If it was he, it seems to me you would have known him when he hammered you."

"How could I, when he was rigged up so different, with his head all covered up?" replied Hasbrook, impatiently. "The man was about the captain's height, but stouter."

"He was dressed for the occasion," added the

sheriff, as he walked to the shore, where the skiff lay.

They dragged it down to the water,—for it was low tide,—and got into it. Beardsley had traced to the cove the print of the heavy boot, which first appeared in some loam under the window where the ruffian had entered Hasbrook's house. He found it in the sand on the shore; and he was satisfied that the perpetrator of the outrage had arrived and departed in a boat. He had obtained from the captain's boot-maker a description of his boots, but none corresponded with those which had made the prints in Northport and Lincolnville.

At the cove all clew to the ruffian had been lost; but now it was regained.

The sheriff paddled the skiff out from the shore in the direction of Seal Island. The water was clear, and they could see the bottom, which they examined very carefully as they proceeded.

"I see it," suddenly exclaimed Hasbrook, as he grasped the boat-hook.

"Lay hold of it," added the sheriff. "I knew I was right."

"I have it.'"

Hasbrook hauled up what appeared to be a bundle of old clothes, and deposited it in the bottom of the skiff. Mr. Beardsley had worked up his case very thoroughly, though it was a little singular that he had not thought to ask Donald any questions; but these investigations had been made when the boat-builder was at home all the time, and the detective did not like to talk about the case any more than was necessary. He had ascertained that Captain Shivernock wore his usual gray suit when Donald saw him after the outrage, and he came to the conclusion that the ruffian had been disguised, for Hasbrook would certainly have known him, even in the dark, in his usual dress. They returned to the shore; and the bundle was lifted, to convey it to the beach.

"It is very heavy," said Hasbrook. "I suppose there is a rock in it to sink it."

"Open it, and throw out the rock," added the sheriff.

Instead of a rock, the weight was half a pig of lead, which had evidently been chopped into two pieces with an axe.

"That's good evidence, for the ballast of the Juno is pig lead," said Beardsley, as he stepped on the beach with the clothes in his hand.

They were spread on the sand, and cc asisted of a large blue woolen frock, such as farmers sometimes wear, a pair of old trousers of very large size, and a pair of heavy cow-hide boots.

"Now I think of it, the man had a frock on," exclaimed Hasbrook.

"That's what made him look stouter than the captain," added Beardsley, as he proceeded to measure one of the boots, and compare it with the notes he had made of the size of the footprints. "It's a plain case; these boots made those tracks."

"And here's the club he pounded me with," said Hasbrook, taking up a heavy stick that had been in the bundle.

"But where in the world did Captain Shivernock get these old duds?" mused the sheriff.

"Of course he procured them to do this job with," replied Hasbrook.

"That's clear enough; but where did they come from? He has covered his tracks so well, that he wouldn't pick these things up near home."

"There comes a boat," said the victim of the outrage, as a sail rounded the point.

"Get out of the way as quick as you can," added the sheriff, in excited tones, as he led the way into the woods near the cove, carrying the wet clothes and boots with him.

"What's the matter now?" demanded Hasbrook.

"That boat is the Juno; Laud Cavendish is in her, and I want to know what he is about. Don't speak a word, or make a particle of noise. If you do, he will sheer off; and I want to see the ballast in that boat."

Laud ran his craft up to the rocks on one side of the cove, where he could land from her; but as it is eleven o'clock, the hour appointed for the regatta, we must return to the city.

CHAPTER XVII.

THE GREAT RACE.

IT was nine o'clock when Donald turned out on the day of the great regatta. He had returned at three in the morning, nearly exhausted by fatigue and anxiety. It was horrible to be suspected of a crime; and bravely as he had carried himself, he was sorely worried. He talked the matter over with his mother and sister while he was eating his breakfast.

"Why should Laud Cavendish charge you with such a wicked deed?" asked his mother.

"To save himself, I suppose," replied Donald. "But he won't make anything by it. He hid those papers in the shop within a day or two, I am sure, for I had my hand in the place where he put them, feeling for a brad-awl I dropped day before yesterday, and I know they were not there then. But he is used up, anyhow, whether we find the box or not, for he tells one story and Captain Shivernock another; and I think Captain Patterdale believes what I say now. But the race comes off to-day, and if I lose it, I am used up too.''

The boat-builder left the house, and went on board of the Maud, which lay off the shop. Samuel Rodman was on deck, and they hoisted the mainsail. The wind had hauled round to the north-west early in the morning, and blew a smashing breeze, just such as Donald wanted for the great occasion. In fact, it blew almost a gale, and the wind came in heavy gusts, which are very trying to the nerves of an inexperienced boatman. The Penobscot, gayly dressed with flags, was moored in her position for the use of the judges.

''We shall not want any kites to-day,'' said Donald, as he made fast the throat halyard.

''No; and you may have to reef this mainsail,'' added Rodman.

''Not at all.''

''But it is flawy.''

''So much the better.''

''Why so?''

''Because a fellow that understands himself and

keeps his eyes wide open has a chance to gain something on the heavy flaws that almost knock a boat over. It makes a sharper game of it."

"But Commodore Montague is up to all those dodges."

"I know he is; but in the other race, he lost half his time by luffing up in a squall."

"But don't you expect a fellow to luff up in a squall?" demanded Rodman.

"If necessary, yes; but the point is, to know when it must be done. If you let off the main-sheet or spill the sail every time a puff comes, you lose time," replied Donald. "I believe in keeping on the safe side; but a fellow may lose the race by dodging every capful of wind that comes. There goes the first gun."

"Let us get into line," added Rodman, as he cast off the moorings and hoisted the jib. "Let her drive."

Donald took the helm, and the Maud shot away like an arrow in the fresh breeze.

"Her sails set beautifully," said the skipper for the occasion; though Rodman was nominally the captain of the yacht, and was so recorded in the books of the club.

"Nothing could be better."

"We shall soon ascertain how stiff she is," added Donald, as a heavy flaw heeled the yacht over, till she buried her rail in the water. "I don't think we shall get anything stronger than that. She goes down just so far, and then the wind seems to slide off. I don't believe you can get her over any farther."

"That's far enough," replied Rodman, holding on, to keep his seat in the standing-room.

The Maud passed under the stern of the judges' yacht, and anchored in the line indicated by the captain of the fleet. The Skylark soon arrived, and took her place next to the Penobscot. In these two yachts all the interest of the occasion centred. The Phantom and the Sea Foam soon came into line; and then it was found that the Christabel had withdrawn, for it blew too hard for her. Mr. Norwood and his son came on board, with Dick Adams, who was to be mate of the Maud, and Kennedy, who was well skilled in sailing a boat. Donald had just the crew he wanted, and he stationed them for the exciting race. Mr. Norwood was to tend the jib-sheets in the standing-room, Kennedy the main sheet, while Dick

20

Adams, Frank Norwood, and Sam Rodman were to cast off the cable and hoist the jib forward.

"Are you all ready, there?" called Donald, raising his voice above the noise made by the banging of the mainsail in the fresh breeze.

"All ready," replied Dick Adams, who was holding the rode with a turn around the bitts.

"Don't let her go till I give the word," added Donald. "I want to fill on the port tack."

"Ay, ay!" shouted Dick; "on the port tack."

This was a very important matter, for the course from the judges' station to Turtle Head would give the yachts the wind on the port quarter; and if any of them came about the wrong way, they would be compelled to gybe, which was not a pleasant operation in so stiff a breeze. Donald kept hold of the main-sheet, and by managing the sail a little, contrived to have the tendency of the Maud in the right direction, so that her sail would fill on the port tack. He saw that Dick Adams had the tender on the port bow, so that the yacht would not run it down when she went off.

"There goes the gun!" shouted Rodman, very much excited as the decisive moment came.

But Dick Adams held on, as he had been instructed to do, and pulled with all his might, in order to throw the head of the Maud in the right direction.

"Hoist the jib!" shouted Donald, when he saw that the yacht was sure to cast on her port tack.

Rodman and Norwood worked lively; and in an instant the jib was up, and Mr. Norwood had gathered up the lee sheet.

"Let go!" added Donald, when he felt that the Maud was in condition to go off lively.

She did go off with a bound and a spring. Donald crowded the helm hard up, so that the Maud wore short around.

"Let off the sheet, lively, Kennedy!" said the skipper. "Ease off the jib-sheet, Mr. Norwood!"

"We shall be afoul of the Phantom!" cried Dick Adams, as he began to run out on the foot-ropes by the bowsprit.

"Lay in, Dick!" shouted Donald. "Don't go out there!"

Dick retraced his steps, and came on deck. The Phantom had not cast in the right direction, and was coming around on the starboard tack, which had very nearly produced a collision with the Maud, the two bowsprits coming within a few inches of each other.

"I was going out to fend off," said Dick, as he came aft, in obedience to orders.

"I was afraid you would be knocked off the bowsprit, which is a bad place to be, when two vessels put their noses together. It was a close shave, but we are all right now," replied the skipper.

"The Sea Foam takes the lead," added Mr. Norwood.

"She had the head end of the line. The Skylark made a good start."

"First rate," said Kennedy. "She couldn't be handled any better than she is."

"We lead her a little," continued Mr. Norwood.

"We had the advantage of her about half a length; as the Sea Foam has a length the best of us."

The yachts were to form the line head to the wind, and this line was diagonal with the course to Turtle Head, so that the Sea Foam, which was farthest from the Penobscot, had really two length's less distance to go in getting to Stubb's

Point Ledge than the Skylark; but this difference was not worth considering in such a breeze, though, if the commodore was beaten by only half a length by the Maud, he intended to claim the race on account of this disparity. The two yachts in which all the interest centred, both obtained a fair start, the Maud a little ahead of her great rival. The Phantom had to come about, and get on the right tack, for Guilford was too careful to gybe in that wind. The Sea Foam got off very well; and Vice Commodore Patterdale was doing his best to make a good show for his yacht, but she held her position only for a moment. The tremendous gusts were too much for Edward's nerves, and he luffed up, in order to escape one. The Maud went tearing by her, with the Skylark over lapping her half a length.

"Haul up the centre-board a little more, Dick," said Donald, who did not bestow a single glance upon his dreaded rival, for all his attention was given to the sailing of the Maud. "A small pull on the jib-sheet, Mr. Norwood, if you please."

"You gained an inch then," said Kennedy, striving to encourage the struggling skipper.

But Donald would not look at the Skylark. He

knew that the shortest distance between two points
was by a straight line; and having taken a tree on
the main land near Castine as his objective point,
he kept it in range with the tompion in the stove-
pipe, and did not permit the Maud to wabble about.
Occasionally the heavy gusts buried the rail in the
brine; but Donald did not permit her to dodge it,
or to deviate from his inflexible straight line.
She went down just so far, and would go no farther; and at these times it was rather difficult to
keep on the seat at the weather side of the standing-room. Dick Adams, Norwood, and Rodman
were placed on deck above the trunk, and had a
comfortable position. The skipper kept his feet
braced against the cleats on the floor, holding on
with both hands at the tiller; for in such a blow,
it was no child's play to steer such a yacht.

"You are gaining on her, Don John," said Mr.
Norwood.

"Do you think so, sir?"

"I know it."

"The end of her bowsprit is about even with
the tip of our main boom," added Kennedy.

"How much fin have we down, Dick?" asked
the skipper.

The mate of the Maud rushed to the cabin, where the line attached to the centre-board was made fast, and reported on its condition.

"Haul up a little more," continued Donald. "Steady! Not the whole of it, but nearly all."

"It is down about six inches now."

"That will do."

For a few moments all hands were still, watching with intense interest the progress of the race. The commodore, in the Skylark, was evidently doing his level best, for he was running away from the Sea Foam and the Phantom.

"Bravo, Don John!" exclaimed the excited Mr. Norwood. "You are a full length ahead! I am willing to sign the contract with Ramsay & Son to build the yacht for me."

"Don't be too fast, sir. We are not out of the woods yet, and shall not be for some time."

"I am satisfied we are going to beat the Skylark."

"Beat her all to pieces!" added Frank Norwood. "She is doing it as easily as though she were used to it."

"I give you the order to build the yacht," said Mr. Norwood.

"Thank you, sir; but I would rather wait till this race is finished before I take the job. We may be beaten yet—badly beaten, too. There are a dozen things that may use us up. The tide is not up, so that I can't play off the dodge I did in the Sea Foam; and if I could, Bob Montague is up to it."

"There is no need of any dodge of any sort," replied Mr. Norwood. "We are beating the Skylark without manœuvring; and that is the fairest way in the world to do it."

"This is plain sailing, sir; and the Skylark's best point is on the wind. For aught I know, the Maud may do the best with a free wind," said Donald; and he had well nigh shuddered when he thought of the difference in yachts in this respect.

"It may be so; but we are at least two lengths ahead of her now."

"Over three," said Kennedy.

"So much the better," laughed Mr. Norwood. "The more we gain with the wind free, the less we shall have to make on the wind."

"But really, sir, this running down here almost before the wind is nothing," protested Donald, who felt that his passenger was indulging in strong expectations, which might not be realized. "The tug of war will come when we go about. We have to beat almost dead to windward; and it may be the Maud has given us her best point off the wind."

"You don't expect her to fail on the wind—do you, Don John."

"No, sir; I don't expect her to fail, for she did first rate yesterday, when we tried her. She looked the breeze almost square in the face; but I can't tell how she will do in comparison with the Skylark. Of course I don't expect the Maud to be beaten; but I don't want you to get your hopes up so high, that you can't bear a disappointment."

"We will try to bear it; but Frank don't want a yacht that is sure to be beaten," added Mr. Norwood.

"Then perhaps it is fortunate I didn't take the job, when you offered to give it to me."

"But I think the Maud will win the race," persisted the confident gentleman.

"So do I; but it is always best to have an anchor out to windward."

"Bully for you, Don John!" shouted Kennedy,

after the yacht had crossed the channel where the sea was very rough and choppy. "You made a good bit in the last quarter of an hour, and we are a dozen lengths ahead of her."

"Surely she can never gain that distance upon us!" exclaimed Mr. Norwood.

"It is quite possible, sir. I have known a boat to get a full mile ahead of another before the wind, and then be beaten by losing it all, and more too, going to windward. I expect better things than that of the Maud; but she may disappoint me. She is only making her reputation now."

Donald watched his "sight" ahead all the time, and had not seen the Skylark for half an hour. The party was silent again for a while, but the Maud dashed furiously on her course, now and then burying her rail, while the water shot up through the lee scupper-holes into the standing-room. But Dick Adams, who was a natural mechanic, was making a pair of plugs to abate this nuisance.

"Turtle Head!" exclaimed Rodman, who, though he had said but little, watched the movements of the yacht with the most intense delight and excitement.

"We are a square quarter of a mile ahead of the Skylark," said Kennedy. "Business will be good with us, Don John, after this."

"Give her a little more main-sheet, Kennedy," was the skipper's reply, as the yacht passed the Head, and he kept her away a little.

"Eleven thirty," mused Mr. Norwood, who had taken out his gold watch, and noted the moment when the Maud passed the headland.

"Now, mind your eye, all hands!" shouted Donald, as the Maud approached the north-east point of Long Island, where he had to change her course from south-east to south, which involved the necessity, with the wind north-west, of gybing, or coming about head to the wind.

It would take a small fraction of a minute to execute the latter manœuvre; and as the sails were now partially sheltered under the lee of the land, the bold skipper determined to gybe. Kennedy had early notice of his intention, and had laid the spare sheet where it would not foul anybody's legs. He hauled in all he could with the help of the mate and others.

"Now, over with it," said Donald, as he put the helm down.

The huge mainsail fluttered and thrashed for an instant, and then flew over. Kennedy, who had been careful to catch a turn in the rope, held fast when the sail "fetched up" on the other tack, and then the yacht rolled her rail under on the port side.

"Let off the sheet, lively!" cried Donald.

"That's what I'm doing," replied the stout ship carpenter, paying off the sheet very rapidly, so as to break the shock.

"Steady! belay! Now draw jib there."

As Dick Adams cast off the weather sheet in the new position, Mr. Norwood hauled in the lee. For a short distance the Maud had the wind on her starboard quarter; then the sheets were hauled in, and she took it on the beam, till she was up with the buoy on Stubbs Point Ledge, which she was to round, leaving it on the port. The ledge was not far from the land, on which was a considerable bluff, so that the wind had not more than half its force. In rounding the buoy, it was necessary to gybe again; and it was done without shaking up the yacht half so much as at the north-east point.

"Now comes the pull," said Donald, as the Maud rounded the buoy. "Stand by your sheets!

Now brace her up! Give her the whole of the board, Dick."

Donald put the helm down; the jib and mainsail were trimmed as flat as it was judicious to have them; and the Maud was close-hauled, standing up to the northward. The skipper was careful not to cramp her by laying too close to the wind. He was an experienced boatman, and he governed himself more by the feeling of the craft under him than by his sight. He could shut his eyes, and tell by the pressure of the tiller in his hand whether she was cramped, or was going along through the water.

"Did you get the time when the Skylark passed the Head, Mr. Norwood?" asked Donald.

"No; you made things so lively, I hadn't time to look," replied the gentleman. "I should like to know just how many minutes we are ahead of her."

"I think I can tell you, sir," added the skipper, with a smile.

"How many?"

"How many do you think, sir?"

"Five or six."

'Not more than one and a half, Mr. Norwood.

Neither yacht has to give the other time, and what we gain belongs to us.''

''I should have thought we were at least five minutes ahead of her.''

''No, sir. Now we have a chance to manœuvre a little,'' added Donald. ''I know just what the commodore will do; he will stand on this tack, when he gets round the buoy, till he is almost up with Brigadier Island; then he will make a long stretch. I shall not do so.''

''Why not?''

''Because, if the wind lessens, he will get under the lee of the land. I shall go just one mile on this tack,'' replied Donald. ''Have you any rubber coats on board, Sam?''

''I have only two.''

''You will want them, for we are beginning to toss the spray about, as though it didn't cost anything.''

It was decidedly damp on the deck of the Maud, for the water thrown up by the waves, dashing against the weather bow, was carried by the gusty wind to the standing-room, drenching those who sat there. Donald and his companions had no fear of salt water, and were just as happy wet to the

skin, as they were when entirely dry, for the
excitement was quite enough to keep them warm,
even in a chill, north-west wind. Half way across
to Brigadier Island, Donald gave the order,
"Ready about," and tacked. As he had predict-
ed, Commodore Montague continued on his course,
almost over to the island, and then came about.
The Maud rushed furiously on her long stretch,
dashing the spray recklessly over her deck, till
she was almost up with the Northport shore, when
she tacked again, and laid her course to windward
of the judges' yacht, as the regulations required.
As she rounded the Penobscot, a gun announced
the arrival of the first yacht. The Maud let off
her sheets, and passed under the stern of the
judges' craft.

"The Maud!" shouted Donald, enraptured with
his victory.

Four minutes and thirty-four seconds later, the
gun announced the arrival of the Skylark. It was
all of twenty minutes later when the Sea Foam
arrived, and half an hour before the Phantom put
in an appearance. There was not a shadow of a
doubt that the Maud had won the great race.

CHAPTER XVIII.

THE HASBROOK OUTRAGE AND OTHER MATTERS.

THE Maud went round to the line, and after picking up her tender and moorings, anchored near the Penobscot.

"There is no doubt now which boat has won the race," said Mr. Norwood.

"None whatever, sir," replied Donald. "The day is ours by as fair a race as ever was sailed. The Maud proved what she could do before we got to Turtle Head; and all the conditions were exactly equal up to that time. If I made anything by manœuvring, it was only when we tacked a mile north of the Head. We have beaten her squarely in a heavy wind; but how she would do compared with the Skylark in a light breeze, is yet to be proved."

" I am satisfied, Don John; and I give you the job to build the Alice, for that is to be the name of Frank's yacht."

"Thank you, sir. I suppose you don't expect to get her out this season."

"No; if he has her by the first of June of next year, it will be soon enough.—I hope you are satisfied with the Maud, Sam," added Mr. Norwood, turning to the owner of the winning craft.

"I ought to be, and I am," replied Rodman.

"You have the fastest yacht in the fleet."

"She won't be when I sail her. The commodore will clean me out every time, if Don John is not at the helm."

"Then there is a capital opportunity for you to improve in the art of sailing a yacht."

"Plenty of room for that," laughed Rodman.

Dick Adams brought the tender alongside, and pulled Mr. Norwood, Rodman, and Donald to the Penobscot.

"I congratulate you, Don John," said Mr. Montague, extending his hand to the boatbuilder. "You have won the race handsomely."

"Thank you, sir."

"It is a double triumph to you, since you both built your yacht, and sailed her," added Mr. Montague.

"It is worth a good deal to me in a business

point of view; for I get a job to build another yacht by it. The firm of Ramsay & Son can't afford to have their boats beaten," laughed Donald. "Here comes Robert."

"I suppose he will not be satisfied with the Skylark, now that she has been so thoroughly whipped," added the commodore's father.

"Perfectly satisfied with her, father. She is as good a boat as she ever was," answered Robert, as he gave his hand to Donald. "You have won the race fairly and handsomely, Don John; and I congratulate you upon your success."

"I thank you, Bob; but I would rather have beaten any other fellow than you," replied Donald.

"I can stand it as well as anybody."

The ladies and gentlemen on board of the Penobscot congratulated the hero of the occasion, and condoled with the commodore, till the last of the fleet arrived. The judges filled out the schedule with the corrected time.

"Captain Rodman, of the Maud," said the chairman; and the owner of the winning yacht stepped forward. "It appears from the schedule that you have made the shortest time, and I have the pleasure of presenting to you the first prize."

"Thank you, sir," replied Rodman, accepting the envelope, which contained the prize of one hundred dollars; "but as it appears that Donald Ramsay sailed the Maud, as well as built her, I shall have the pleasure of presenting it to him."

A round of hearty applause followed this little speech, which ended in three cheers for the captain of the Maud, and three more for her builder.

"I can't take that," said Donald, declining to receive the envelope.

"But you must take it. I will hand you over to Mr. Deputy Sheriff Beardsley, who, I see, is coming up the bay in the Juno."

"It don't belong to me. I am not the owner of the Maud," protested Donald.

"Take it! take it!" shouted one and another of the interested spectators, until nearly all of them had expressed their opinion in this way.

Thus overborne, the boat-builder took the envelope, though his pride revolted.

"Commodore Montague, it appears that the Skylark made the next best time, and I have the pleasure of presenting to you the second prize."

"Which I devote to the club for the building fund."

The members heartily applauded this disposal of the money.

"I will give the other prize to the club for the same purpose," added Donald.

"Impossible!" exclaimed Commodore Montague. "The fund is completed, and the donation cannot be accepted."

"No! No!" shouted the members.

"The fifty dollars I added to the fund just makes up the sum necessary to pay for the club-house on Turtle Head, which is to be only a shanty; so you can't play that game on us, Don John."

Donald was compelled to submit; and he transferred the hundred dollars to his pocket-book.

"I am so glad you won the race, Don John!" said Nellie Patterdale. "Everybody said you sailed the Maud splendidly."

"Thank you, Nellie; your praise is worth more to me than that of all the others," replied Donald, blushing deeply; but I must do him the justice to say that, if he had not been laboring under intense excitement, he would not have made so palpable a speech to her.

Nellie blushed too; but she was not angry,

though her father might have been, if he had heard the remark.

"Is Captain Patterdale on board?" shouted Mr. Beardsley, as the Juno ran under the stern of the Penobscot.

"Here," replied the captain.

"I want to see you and Don John," added the officer.

The business of the race was finished, and the Maud conveyed Captain Patterdale, his daughter, and Donald to the shore. Laud Cavendish was in the Juno, and so was Hasbrook; but none of the party knew what had transpired at Saturday Cove during the forenoon.

"I will be at your house in half an hour, Captain Patterdale," said Donald, as they landed. "I am wet to the skin, and I want to put on dry clothes."

Mr. Beardsley had proposed the place of meeting; and the boat-builder hastened home. In a few minutes he had put himself inside a dry suit of clothes. Then he went to the shop, and wrote a brief note to Captain Shivernock, in which he enclosed sixty dollars, explaining that as he had been unable to "keep still with his tongue," he could not keep the money. He also added, that he should send him the amount received for the Juno when he obtained the bills from Captain Patterdale, who had a part of them. Sealing this note in an envelope, he called at the house of the strange man, on his way to the place of meeting. Mrs. Sykes said that Captain Shivernock was in his library.

"Please to give him this; and if he wishes to see me, I shall be at Captain Patterdale's house for an hour or two," continued Donald; and without giving the housekeeper time to reply, he hastened off, confident there would be a storm as soon as the eccentric opened the note.

In the library of the elegant mansion, he found the party who had been in the Juno, with Captain Patterdale and Nellie. On the desk was the tin box, the paint on the outside stained with yellow loam. Laud Cavendish looked as though life was a burden to him, and Donald readily comprehended the situation.

"We have found the tin box," said Mr. Beardsley, with a smile, as the boat-builder was admitted.

"Where did you find it?"

"Laud had it in his hand down at Saturday Cove. While I was looking up the Hasbrook affair, our friend here landed from the Juno, and was walking towards the woods, when he walked into me. He owns up to everything."

"Then I hope you are satisfied that I had nothing to do with the box."

"Of course we are," interposed Captain Patterdale. "It certainly looked bad for you at one time, Don John."

"I know it did, sir," added Donald.

"But I could not really believe that you would do such a thing," said the captain.

"I knew he wouldn't," exclaimed Nellie.

"Laud says he buried the box on Turtle Head, just where you said, and only removed it yesterday, when he put the notes under the sill in your shop," continued Mr. Beardsley.

"What did you do that for, Laud?" asked Donald, turning to the culprit.

"You promised not to tell where I got the money to pay for the Juno. You went back on me," pleaded Laud.

"I told you I wouldn't tell if everything was all right. When it appeared that the mended bill was not all right, I mentioned your name, but not till then.''

"That is so,'' added the nabob. "Now, Laud, did Captain Shivernock pay you any money?''

"No, sir,'' replied Laud, who had concluded to tell the whole truth, hoping it would go easier with him if he did so.

"Where did you get the mended bill you paid Don John?''

"From the tin trunk.''

"Why did you say that Captain Shivernock gave you the money you paid for the Juno?''

"I couldn't account for it in any other way. I knew the captain threw his money around very loosely, and I didn't think any one would ask him if he gave me the money. If any one did, he wouldn't answer.''

"But he did answer, and said he gave you the money.''

"He told me he would say so, when I went to see him a fortnight ago.''

"Why did you go to see him?''

Laud glanced at Donald with a faint smile on his haggard face.

"Don John told me Captain Shivernock had a secret he wanted to keep."

"I told you so!" exclaimed Donald.

"You did; but you thought I knew the secret," answered Laud. "You told me the captain had given me the money not to tell that I had seen him near Saturday Cove on the morning after the Hasbrook affair."

"I remember now," said Donald. "Captain Shivernock gave me sixty dollars, and then gave me the Juno, for which I understood that I was not to say I had seen him that day. I refused to sell the boat to Laud till he told me where he got the money. When he told me the captain had given it to him, and would not say what for, I concluded his case was just the same as my own. After I left the captain, he stood over to the Northport shore, and Laud went over there soon after. I was sure that they met."

"We didn't meet; and I did not see Captain Shivernock that day," Laud explained.

"I supposed he had; I spoke to Laud just as though he had, and he didn't deny that he had seen him."

"Of course I didn't. Don John made my story good, and I was willing to stick to it."

"But you did not stick to it," added the nabob. "You said you had paid no money to Don John."

"I will tell you how that was. When I got the secret out of Don John, I went to the captain with it. He asked me if I wanted to black-mail him. I told him no. Then I spoke to him about the tin trunk you had lost, and said one of the bills had been traced to me. I made up a story to show where I got the bill; but the man that gave it to me had gone, and I didn't even know his name. He had some bills just like that mended one; and when I told him what my trouble was, he promised to say that he had given me the bill; and then he laughed as I never saw a man laugh before."

"What was he laughing at?" asked the sheriff.

"He went off early the next morning, and I suppose he was laughing to think what a joke he was playing upon me, for he was not to be in town when wanted to get me out of trouble."

"He did say he let you have the use of the Juno for taking care of her, and that he gave you the money, though he wouldn't indicate what it was for," added the officer.

"I thought he was fooling me, and I didn't 'pend on him."

"That's Captain Shivernock," said the good nabob, as the party in the library were startled by a violent ring at the door.

It was the strange man. He was admitted by Nellie. He stalked up to Donald, his face red with wrath, and dashed the letter and bills into his face, crumpled up into a ball.

"You canting little monkey! What have you been doing?" roared he.

"Since I could not do what you wished me to do, I have returned your money," replied Donald, rising from his chair, for he feared the captain intended to assault him.

"Have you disobeyed my orders, you whelp?"

"I have; for I told you I should tell no lies."

"I'll break every bone in your body for this!" howled Captain Shivernock.

"Not yet, captain," interposed Mr. Beardsley. "You may have something else to break before you do that job."

"Who are you?" demanded the wicked nabob, with what was intended as a withering sneer; but no one wilted under it.

"A deputy sheriff of Waldo County, at your service; and I have a warrant for your arrest."

"For my arrest!" gasped Captain Shivernock, dismounting from his high horse, for he had a wholesome fear of the penalties of violated law.

"Here is the document," added the sheriff, producing a paper.

"For what?"

"For breaking and entering in the night time, in the first place, and for an aggravated assault on Jacob Hasbrook in the second."

"What assault? You can't prove it."

"Yes, we can; we went a fishing down in Saturday Cove this morning, and we caught a bundle, containing a pair of boots, a blue frock, and other articles, including the stick the assault was committed with. They were sunk with half a pig of lead, the other half of which I found in the Juno. I hope you are satisfied."

"No, I'm not. I didn't leave my house till four o'clock that morning; and I can prove it."

"You will have an opportunity to do so in court."

The wicked nabob was silent.

"I was bound to follow this thing up to the bitter end," said Hasbrook, rejoiced at the detection of the wretch.

"You got what you deserved, you miserable, canting villain!" roared the captain. "You cheated me out of a thousand dollars, by giving me an indorser you knew wasn't worth a dollar."

"But I meant to pay you. I pay my debts. I appeal to Captain Patterdale to say whether I do or not."

"I think you do when it is for your interest to do so, or when you can't help it," added the good nabob, candidly. "I suppose you know Mr. Laud Cavendish, captain?"

"I do," growled the rich culprit. "He is the fellow that saved a man's life down at Haddock Ledge; a man he hadn't been introduced to, who gave him a pile of money for the job, but didn't give him his name."

"But, Captain Shivernock, you said you gave him some money, and you didn't tell us what you gave it to him for," added Beardsley.

"That was my joke."

"We do not see the point of it."

"I only wanted the privilege of proving to Captain Patterdale that he was mistaken about the bill, by showing him three more just like it."

"How do you fold your money, Captain Shivernock?" asked the nabob.

"None of your business, you canting psalm-singer."

"I shall be obliged to commit you," said the sheriff, sharply.

"Commit me!' howled the wicked nabob. "I should like to see you do it."

"You shall have that satisfaction. If you give me any trouble about it, I shall have to put these things on," added the sheriff, taking from his pocket a pair of handcuffs.

The culprit withered at the sight of the irons. He and Laud both walked to the county jail, where they were locked up. Of course the imprisonment of such a man as the wicked nabob caused a sensation; but there was no one to object. He was willing to pay any sum of money to get out of the scrape; but the majesty of the law must be vindicated, and there was a contest between money and justice. He obtained bail by depositing the large amount required in the hands of two men, whom his well-feed lawyer procured. Between two days he left the city; but Beardsley kept the run of him, and when he was wanted for trial, he was brought back from a western state.

On the trial a desperate attempt was made to break down the witnesses; but it failed. The first for the defence was Mrs. Sykes; but her evidence was not what had been expected of her. She had told, and repeated the lie, that the captain left his house at four o'clock on the morning after the outrage; but in court, and under oath, she would not perjure herself. She declared that the defendant had left home about eleven o'clock in the evening, dressed in her husband's blue frock, boots, and hat. Mr. Sykes, after his wife had told the whole truth, was afraid to testify as he had said he should do. A conviction followed; and the prisoner was sentenced to the state prison for ten years. He was overwhelmed by this result. He swore like a pirate, and then he wept like a child; but he was sent to Thomaston, and put to hard work.

Laud pleaded guilty, and was sent to the same institution for a year. There was hope of him; for if he could get rid of his silly vanity, and go to work, he might be saved from a lifetime of crime.

Donald came out of the fire without the stain of smoke upon him. After the great race, as Mr. Norwood was in no hurry for the Alice, he went on the long cruise with the fleet, in the Sea Foam. They coasted along the shore as far as Portland, visiting the principal places on the seaboard. On the cruise down Donald "coached" his friend, Ned Patterdale, in the art of sailing; and on the return he rendered the same service to Rodman. Both of them proved to be apt scholars; and after long practice, they were able to bring out the speed of their yachts, and stood a fair chance in a regatta.

On the cruise, the yachts were racing all the time when under way, but the results were by no means uniform. When Donald sailed the Maud, she beat the Skylark; but when Rodman skippered her himself, the commodore outsailed him. The Maud beat the Sea Foam, as a general rule; but one day Robert Montague sailed the latter, and the former was beaten.

"Don John, I don't know yet which is the fastest craft in the fleet," said Commodore Montague, as they were seated on Manheigan Island, looking down upon the fleet anchored below them.

"I thought you did, Bob," laughed Donald.

"No, I don't. I have come to the conclusion that you can sail a yacht better than I can, and that is the reason that you beat me in the Maud, as you did in the Sea Foam."

"No, no!" replied Donald. "I am sure I can't sail a boat any better than you can."

"I can outsail any boat in the fleet when you are ashore."

"We can easily settle the matter, Bob."

"How?"

"You shall sail the Maud, and I will sail the Skylark. If the difference is in the skippers, we shall come in about even. If the Maud is the better sailer, you will beat me."

"Good! I'll do it."

"You will do your best in the Maud—won't you?"

"Certainly; and you will do the same in the Skylark."

"To be sure. We will sail around Matinicus Rock and back."

The terms of the race were agreed upon, and the interest of the whole club was excited. The party went on board the fleet, and the two yachts were

moored in line. At the firing of the gun on board
the Sea Foam, they run up their jibs and got
a good start. The wind was west, a lively breeze,
but not heavy. Each yacht carried her large
gaff-topsail and the balloon-jib. The course was
about forty miles, the return from the rock
being a beat dead to windward. Robert and
Donald each did his best, and the Maud came in
twelve minutes ahead of the Skylark.

"I am satisfied now," said Robert, when they
met after the race.

"I was satisfied before," laughed Donald. "I
was confident the Maud was faster than the Skylark or the Sea Foam."

"I agree with you now; and I have more respect
for myself than I had before, for I thought it was
you, and not the Maud, which had beaten me,"
added Robert. "I have also a very high respect
for the firm of Ramsay & Son."

The members of the club enjoyed the excursion
exceedingly; and on their return it was decided
to repeat it the next year, if not before. The
club-house on Turtle Head was finished when the
fleet arrived at Belfast; and during the rest of the
vacation, the yachts remained in the bay. They

MAUD.

had chowders and fries at the Head, to which the ladies were invited; and Donald made himself as agreeable as possible to Miss Nellie on these occasions. Possibly her father and mother had some objections to this continued and increasing intimacy; if they had, they did not mention them. They were compelled to acknowledge, when they talked the matter over between themselves, that Donald Ramsay was an honest, intelligent, noble young man, with high aims and pure principles, and that these qualifications were infinitely preferable to wealth without them; and they tacitly permitted the affair to take its natural course, as I have no doubt it will. Certainly the young people were very devoted to each other; and though they are too young to think of anything but friendship, it will end in a wedding.

In the autumn, after the frame of the Alice was all set up, Barbara obtained a situation as a teacher in one of the public schools, and added her salary to the income of the boat-builder. The family lived well, and were happy in each other. After the boating season closed, the yacht club hired apartments, in which a library and reading-room were fitted up; and the members not only enjoyed the meetings every week, but they profited by their reading and their study. Donald is still an honored and useful member, and people say that, by and by, when the country regains her mercantile marine, he will be a ship-builder, and not, as now, THE YOUNG BOAT-BUILDER.

LEE & SHEPARD'S

LIST OF

JUVENILE PUBLICATIONS.

OLIVER OPTIC'S BOOKS.

Each Set in a neat Box with Illuminated Titles.

Army and Navy Stories. A Library for Young and Old, in 6 volumes. 16mo. Illustrated. Per vol........$1 50

The Soldier Boy.   The Yankee Middy.
The Sailor Boy.   Fighting Joe.
The Young Lieutenant.   Brave Old Salt.

Famous "Boat-Club" Series. A Library for Young People. Handsomely Illustrated. Six volumes, in neat box. Per vol 1 25

The Boat Club ; or, The Bunkers of Rippleton.
All Aboard ; or, Life on the Lake.
Now or Never ; or, The Adventures of Bobby Bright.
Try Again ; or, The Trials and Triumphs of Harry West.
Poor and Proud ; or, The Fortunes of Katy Redburn.
Little by Little ; or, The Cruise of the Flyaway.

Lake Shore Series, The. Six volumes. Illustrated. In neat box. Per vol 1 25

Through by Daylight ; or, The Young Engineer of the Lake Shore Railroad.
Lightning Express ; or, The Rival Academies.
On Time , or, The Young Captain of the Ucayga Steamer.
Switch Off ; or, The War of the Students.
Break Up ; or, The Young Peacemakers.
Bear and Forbear ; or, The Young Skipper of Lake Ucayga.

Soldier Boy Series, The. Three volumes, in neat box. Illustrated. Per vol........................... 1 50

The Soldier Boy ; or, Tom Somers in the Army.
The Young Lieutenant ; or, The Adventures of an Army Officer.
Fighting Joe ; or, The Fortunes of a Staff Officer.

Sailor Boy Series, The. Three volumes in neat box. Illustrated. Per vol................................. 1 50

The Sailor Boy ; or, Jack Somers in the Navy.
The Yankee Middy ; or, Adventures of a Naval Officer.
Brave Old Salt ; or, Life on the Quarter-Deck.

Starry Flag Series, The. Six volumes. Illustrated. Per vol...................................... 1 25

The Starry Flag ; or, The Young Fisherman of Cape Ann.
Breaking Away ; or, The Fortunes of a Student.
Seek and Find ; or, The Adventures of a Smart Boy.
Freaks of Fortune ; or, Half Round the World.
Make or Break ; or, The Rich Man's Daughter.
Down the River ; or, Buck Bradford and the Tyrants.

The Household Library. 3 volumes. Illustrated. Per volume................................. 1 50

Living too Fast.   In Doors and Out.
The Way of the World.

Way of the World, The. By William T. Adams (Oliver Optic)...............................12mo 1 50

Woodville Stories. Uniform with Library for Young People. Six volumes. Illustrated. Per vol.....16mo 1 25

Rich and Humble ; or, The Mission of Bertha Grant.
In School and Out ; or, The Conquest of Richard Grant.
Watch and Wait ; or, The Young Fugitives.
Work and Win ; or, Noddy Newman on a Cruise.
Hope and Have ; or, Fanny Grant among the Indians.
Haste and Waste ; or, The Young Pilot of Lake Champlain.

Yacht Club Series. Uniform with the ever popular "Boat Club" Series. Completed in six vols. Illustrated. Per vol.................................... ... .16mo 1 50

Little Bobtail ; or, The Wreck of the Penobscot.
The Yacht Club ; or, The Young Boat Builders.
Money Maker ; or, The Victory of the Basilisk.
The Coming Wave ; or, The Treasure of High Rock.
The Dorcas Club ; or, Our Girls Afloat.
Ocean Born ; or, The Cruise of the Clubs.

Onward and Upward Series, The. Complete in six volumes. Illustrated. In neat box. Per vol.......... 1 25

Field and Forest ; or, The Fortunes of a Farmer.
Plane and Plank ; or, The Mishaps of a Mechanic.
Desk and Debit ; or, The Catastrophes of a Clerk.
Cringle and Cross-Tree ; or, The Sea Swashes of a Sailor.
Bivouac and Battle ; or, The Struggles of a Soldier.
Sea and Shore ; or, The Tramps of a Traveller.

Young America Abroad Series. A Library of Travel and Adventure in Foreign Lands. Illustrated by Nast, Stevens, Perkins, and others. Per vol. 16mo 1 50

First Series.

Outward Bound ; or, Young America Afloat.
Shamrock and Thistle ; or, Young America in Ireland and Scotland.
Red Cross ; or, Young America in England and Wales.
Dikes and Ditches , or, Young America in Holland and Belgium.
Palace and Cottage; or, Young America in France and Switzerland.
Down the Rhine ; or, Young America in Germany. .

Second Series.

Up the Baltic ; or, Young America in Norway, Sweden, and Denmark.
Northern Lands ; or, Young America in Russia and Prussia.
Cross and Crescent ; or, Young America in Turkey and Greece.
Sunny Shores ; or, Young America in Italy and Austria.
Vine and Olive ; or, Young America in Spain and Portugal.
Isles of the Sea ; or, Young America Homeward Bound.

Riverdale Stories. Twelve volumes. A New Edition. Profusely Illustrated from new designs by Billings. In neat box. Per vol.........................

Little Merchant.	Proud and Lazy.
Young Voyagers.	Careless Kate.
Robinson Crusoe, Jr.	Christmas Gift.
Dolly and I.	The Picnic Party.
Uncle Ben.	The Gold Thimble.
Birthday Party.	The Do-Somethings.

Riverdale Story Books. Six volumes, in neat box Cloth. Per vol..........................

Little Merchant.	Proud and Lazy.
Young Voyagers.	Careless Kate.
Dolly and I.	Robinson Crusoe, Jr.

Flora Lee Story Books. Six volumes in neat box. Cloth. Per vol..........................

Christmas Gift.	The Picnic Party.
Uncle Ben.	The Gold Thimble.
Birthday Party.	The Do-Somethings.

Great Western Series, The. Six volumes. Illustrated. Per vol.................................... I 50

Going West; or, The Perils of a Poor Boy.
Out West; or, Roughing it on the Great Lakes.
Lake Breezes.

Our Boys' and Girls' Offering. Containing Oliver Optic's popular Story, Ocean Born; or, The Cruise of the Clubs; Stories of the Seas, Tales of Wonder, Records of Travel, &c. Edited by Oliver Optic. Profusely Illustrated. Covers printed in Colors. 8vo........... I 50

Our Boys' and Girls' Souvenir. Containing Oliver Optic's Popular Story, Going West; or, The Perils of a Poor Boy; Stories of the Sea, Tales of Wonder, Records of Travel, &c. Edited by Oliver Optic. With numerous full-page and letter-press Engravings. Covers printed in Colors. 8vo.................................... I 50

ELIJAH KELLOGG'S NEW BOOKS.

JOHN GODSOE'S LEGACY. 16mo. Illustrated. $1.25.

THE FISHER BOYS OF PLEASANT COVE. 16mo. Illustrated. $1.25. Completing THE PLEASANT COVE SERIES.

THE PLEASANT COVE SERIES. Five vols. Illustrated. Per vol., $1.25.

>   1. ARTHUR BROWN.
>   2. THE YOUNG DELIVERERS.
>   3. THE CRUISE OF THE CASCO.
>   4. THE CHILD OF THE ISLAND GLEN.
>   5. JOHN GODSOE'S LEGACY.
>   6. FISHER BOYS OF PLEASANT COVE.

THE TURNING OF THE TIDE; OR, RADCLIFFE RICH AND HIS PATIENTS. 16mo. Illustrated. $1.25.

A STOUT HEART; OR, THE STUDENT FROM OVER THE SEA. 16mo. Illustrated. Cloth. $1.25.

THE WHISPERING PINE SERIES. 6 vols. Illustrated. Per vol., $1.25.

>   1. THE SPARK OF GENIUS.
>   2. THE SOPHOMORES OF RADCLIFFE.
>   3. THE WHISPERING PINE.
>   4. WINNING HIS SPURS.
>   5. THE TURNING OF THE TIDE.
>   6. A STOUT HEART.

"Mr. Kellogg has made himself a great favorite with young people by the number and variety of adventures which he manages to pack into a book; and to the parents by the excellent precepts which he inculcates."

BY SOPHIE MAY.

Little Prudy's Flyaway Series. By the author of "Dotty Dimple Stories," and "Little Prudy Stories." Complete in six volumes. Illustrated. Per vol....... **75**

Little Folks Astray.
Prudy Keeping House.
Aunt Madge's Story.
Little Grandmother.
Little Grandfather.
Miss Thistledown.

Little Prudy Stories. By Sophie May. Complete. Six volumes, handsomely illustrated, in a neat box. Per vol.................................... **75**

Little Prudy.
Little Prudy's Sister Susy.
Little Prudy's Captain Horace.
Little Prudy's Cousin Grace.
Little Prudy's Story Book.
Little Prudy's Dotty Dimple.

Dotty Dimple Stories. By Sophie May, author of Little Prudy. Complete in six volumes. Illustrated. Per vol.................................... **75**

Dotty Dimple at her Grandmother's.
Dotty Dimple at Home.
Dotty Dimple out West.
Dotty Dimple at Play.
Dotty Dimple at School.
Dotty Dimple's Flyaway.

The Quinnebassett Girls. 16mo. Illustrated...... 1 50

The Doctor's Daughter. 16mo. Illustrated... ..... 1 50
Our Helen. 16mo. Illustrated..................... 1 50
The Asbury Twins. 16mo. Illustrated............. 1 5c

Flaxie Frizzle Stories. To be completed in six volumes. Illustrated. Per vol................................... **75**

Flaxie Frizzle.
Flaxie Frizzle and Doctor Papa.
Little Pitchers.

Young Dodge Club, The. By James De Mille, author of the B. O. W. C. Stories. Complete in three vols. Illustrated. Per volume 1 50

> Among the Brigands.   The Seven Hills.
> The Winged Lion.

Hunter's Library, The. 5 volumes. Illustrated. Per volume.............. .... 1 50

Australian Wanderers. The Adventures of Capt. Spencer and his Horse and Dog in the Wilds of Australia.
The African Crusoes. The Adventures of Carlos and Antonio in the Wilds of Africa.
Anecdotes of Animals, with their Habits, Instincts, &c., &c.
Anecdotes of Birds, Fishes, Reptiles, &c., their Habits and Instincts.
A Thousand Miles' Walk Across South America, over the Pampas and the Andes.

Little People of God, and what the Poets have said of them. By Mrs. George L. Austin. 4to. Illustrated... 2 00

Frontier Series, The. Five volumes. Illustrated. Per vol..................................... 1 25

Twelve Nights in the Hunters' Camp.
A Thousand Miles' Walk Across South America.
The Cabin on the Prairie.
Planting the Wilderness.
The Young Pioneers of the Northwest.

Helping Hand Series. By May Mannering. Complete in six vols. Illustrated. Per volume........... 1 00

> Climbing the Rope.   The Little Spaniard.
> Billy Grimes's Favorite.   ·   Salt-water Dick.
> The Cruise of the Dashaway.   Little Maid of Oxbow.
> An entirely new edition.

Cast Away in the Cold. An Old Man's Story of a Young Man's Adventures. By Dr. Isaac I. Hayes. 1 volume. Illustrated..................................... 1.25

Vacation Story-Books. For Boys and Girls. Finely Illustrated from designs by Hoppin and others. Six volumes, square 16mo. In neat box. Per volume.... 80

> Worth not Wealth.   Karl Keigler.
> Country Life.   Walter Seyton.
> The Charm.   Holidays at Chestnut Hill.

Winwood Cliff Stories. By the Rev. Daniel Wise, D.D., author of the "Glen Morris Stories." To be completed in six volumes. Per volume............... 1 00

Winwood Cliff; or, Oscar, The Sailor's Son.
Ben Blinker; or, Maggie's Golden Motto, and what it did for her Brother.
A new volume in Press.

Young Trail-Hunters' Series, The. By Samuel Woodworth Cozzens. 12mo. Per vol..................... 1 00

Young Silver Seekers, The; or, Hal and Ned in Sonora. (In press.)
Crossing the Quicksands; or, The Veritable Adventures of Hal and Ned upon the Pacific Slope. 16mo. Illustrated. 317 pp.. 1 00
The Young Trail-Hunters; or, The Wild Riders of the Plains. 12mo. Illustrated. 205 pp.................. 1 00

Battles at Home. By Mary G. Darling. Illustrated. 12mo.. 1 00

In the World. By Mary G. Darling. Illustrated. 12mo. 1 00

Golden Hair. A Story of the Pilgrims. By Sir Lascelles Wraxhall, Bart. 12mo. Illustrated.................. 1.00

Snip and Whip, and some other Boys. By Elizabeth A. Davis. 16mo. Cloth. Illustrated.................... 1.25

Sunnybank Stories. Twelve volumes. Compiled by Rev. Asa Bullard, editor of the "Well-Spring." Profusely Illustrated. 32mo. Bound in high colors, and put in a neat box. Per volume....................... 25

Uncle Henry's Stories.	Aunt Lizzie's Stories.
Dog Stories.	Mother's Stories.
Stories for Alice.	Grandpa's Stories.
My Teacher's Gem.	The Good Scholar.
The Scholar's Welcome.	The Lighthouse.
Going to School.	Reward of Merit.

Sunnybank Stories. Six volumes. Compiled by Rev. Asa Bullard. Profusely Illustrated. 32mo. Bound in high colors, and put up in a neat box. Per volume.... 25

Uncle Henry's Stories.	Aunt Lizzie's Stories.
Dog Stories.	Mother's Stories.
Stories for Alice.	Grandpa's Stories.

Shady Dell Stories. Six volumes. Compiled by Rev. Asa Bullard, editor of the " Well-Spring." Profusely Illustrated. 32mo. Bound in high colors, and put up in a neat box (to match the Sunnybank Stories). Per volume 25

My Teacher's Gem.	The Good Scholar.
The Scholar's Welcome.	The Lighthouse.
Going to School.	Reward of Merit.

Tone Masters, The. A Musical Series for the Young. By the author of " The Soprano," &c. 16mo. Illustrated. Per volume................................. 1 25

Mozart and Mendelssohn.	Handel and Haydn.
Bach and Beethoven.	

Twilight Stories. By Mrs. Follen. Twelve volumes. 4to. Illustrated. Per volume....................... 50

Travellers' Stories.	The Talkative Wig.
True Stories about Dogs.	What Animals do and say.
Made-Up Stories.	Two Festivals.
Peddler of Dust Sticks.	Conscience.
When I was a Girl.	Piccolissima.
Who speaks Next?	Little Songs.

Maidenhood Series. 12mo. Illustrated.

Seven Daughters. By Miss A. M. Douglas..............	1 50
Running to Waste : The Story of a Tomboy. By Geo. M. Baker....................................	1 50
Our Helen. By Sophie May........................	1 75
That Queer Girl. By Virginia F. Townsend...........	1 50
The Asbury Twins. By Sophie May..................	1 75
Daisy Travers ; or, The Girls of Hive Hall. By Adelaide F. Samuels..................................	1 50

Amateur Drama Series. By Geo. M. Baker. 6 volumes. Illustrated. Per vol.......................... 1 50

Amateur Dramas.	The Drawing-Room Stage.
The Mimic Stage.	The Exhibition Drama.
The Social Stage.	Handy Dramas.

Eminent Statesmen. The Young American's Library of Eminent Statesmen. Uniform with the Young American's Library of Famous Generals. Six volumes, handsomely illustrated, in neat box. (New edition.) Per volume.................................... 1 25

Benjamin Franklin.	William Penn.
Daniel Webster.	Henry Clay.
Daring Deeds.	Noble Deeds.

Famous Generals. The Young American's Library of Famous Generals. A useful and attractive series of books for Boys. Six volumes, handsomely illustrated, in neat box. (New edition.) Per vol................. 1 25

General Washington.	General Lafayette.
General Taylor.	General Marion.
General Jackson.	Napoleon Bonaparte.

Springdale Stories. By Mrs. S. B. C. Samuels. Six volumes. Illustrated. Per volume................... 75

Obeying the Golden Rule.	The Smuggler's Cave.
The Shipwrecked Girl.	Under the Sea.
Nettie's Trial.	The Burning Prairie.

Charley Roberts Series. By Miss Louise M. Thurston. To be completed in six volumes. Per vol........ 1 00

How Charlie Roberts became a Man.
How Eva Roberts gained her Education.
Home in the West.
Children of Amity Court.

Crusoe Library. An attractive series for Young and Old. Six volumes. Illustrated. In neat box. Per vol. 1 50

Robinson Crusoe.
Arabian Nights.
Arctic Crusoe.
Young Crusoe.
Prairie Crusoe.
Willis the Pilot.

Dick and Daisy Series. By Miss Adelaide F. Samuels. Four volumes. Illustrated. Per vol............ 50

Adrift in the World ; or, Dick and Daisy's Early Days.
Fighting the Battle ; or, Dick and Daisy's City Life.
Saved from the Street ; or, Dick and Daisy's protégés.
Grandfather Milly's Luck ; or, Dick and Daisy's Reward.

Dick Travers Abroad Series: By Miss Adelaide F. Samuels. Four volumes. Illustrated. Per vol........ 50

Little Cricket ; or, Dick Travers in London.
Palm Land ; or, Dick Travers in the Chagos Islands.
The Lost Tar ; or, Dick Travers in Africa.
On the Wave ; or, Dick Travers aboard the Happy Jack.
The Turning of the Tide ; or, Radcliffe Rich and his Patients.
Winning his Spurs ; or, Henry Morton's First Trial.

Girlhood Series, The. Comprising six volumes. 12mo. Illustrated.. 1 50

An American Girl Abroad. By Miss Adeline Trafton.
The Doctor's Daughter. By Sophie May.
Sallie Williams, The Mountain Girl. By Mrs. E. D. Cheney.
Only Girls. By Virginia F. Townsend.
Lottie Eames ; or, Do Your Best, and Leave the Rest.
Rhoda Thornton's Girlhood. By Mrs. Mary E. Pratt.

BY J. T. TROWBRIDGE.

His Own Master. 16mo. Cloth. Illustrated. (In press.) 1 25

Bound in Honor; or, Boys will be Boys. 16mo. Cloth. Illustrated.. 1 25

MISCELLANEOUS.

Alden Series. By Joseph Alden, D.D. 4 vols. Illustrated. Per vol............................... ..... 5c

> The Cardinal Flower.   Henry Ashton.
> The Lost Lamb.   The Light-hearted Girl.

Baby Ballad Series. (In press.) Three volumes. Illustrated. 4to. Per vol.............................. 1 00

> Baby Ballads.   By Uno.
> Little Songs.   By Mrs. Follen.
> New Songs for Little People.   By Mrs. Anderson.

Beckoning Series. By Paul Cobden.   To be completed in six volumes.   Illustrated.   Per vol.................. 1 25

> Who will Win ?   Good Luck.
> Going on a Mission.   Take a Peep.
> The Turning Wheel.   (Another in preparation.)

Blue Jacket Series. Six vols. 12mo. Illustrated. Per vol.. 1.5c

> Swiss Family Robinson.   Gulliver's Travels.
> Willis the Pilot.   The Arctic Crusoe.
> The Prairie Crusoe.   The Young Crusoe.

Celesta Stories, The. By Mrs. E. M. Berry. 16mo. Illustrated. Per vol................................... 1 00

> Celesta.   The Crook Straightened.
> Crooked and Straight.